Andy Anders
and the Rebel Spies

An Andy Anders Civil War Adventure

by Allen Alright

This book is Dedicated to

CATS Hunter

Acknowledgements

I wish to thank my loving wife, Gayle,

for putting up with me during NaNoWriMo,

and afterwards for all of her patience and help.

And to all my friends who helped review and
beta-read this book for me, especially:

Jim and Lou

Andy Anders
and the Rebel Spies

An Andy Anders Civil War Adventure

by Allen Alright

CONTENTS

Contents

Map of Mercyville, Connecticut 1860   Plate 1 of 2
(Souther View from North Notch Mountain)

Commissioned by the Right Honorable Mayor Aloysius T. Katz

Plate 2 of 2

Map of Mercyville, Connecticut 1860
(Souther View from North Notch Mountain)

Commissioned by the Right Honorable Mayor Aloysius T. Katz

THE BOY IN THE ATTIC

It all started with a knock on the front door of the Mercyville Inn. Aunt Abby was not expecting anyone to come knocking on the front door of the inn this early in the morning. After all, meeting members should not be arriving for at least another half hour. Nervously, Abby put her meeting sign down on the stand in the corner and straightened her apron.

Opening the front door of the inn, Abby discovered ten-year-old Andy Anders standing there with two large envelops pinned to his coat lapel, and he carried a small carpetbag, "Oh! Hi, Andy! How can I help you?"

"Hi, Aunt Abby! My Mom's attorney told me…" He stopped talking to scratch his jaw and think for a moment. "Mister Fishkill, said to come here to live with you. I think it means we are now related. He said you would know all about it."

She poked her head out the front door and nervously looked around. No one else was there, "Andy, where's your Mom?"

Uncomfortably answering her, "Aunt Abby, Mom's dead and buried. The consumption got her three days ago. Oh, I almost forgot. These letters are for you."

From his coat lapel, he unpinned the two envelopes and handed them over to his aunt, who was not really his aunt, but he still called her aunt. "Ah, Mister Fishkill said it's all in these letters, and to give them to you."

She opened and read the attorney's letter:

"Andrew Adams Anders is to be immediately placed in the charge of his not aunt, Mrs. Abigale Bennington Cardstacker residing in Mercyville, Connecticut, widow, and owner of the Mercyville Inn. She is aware of my wishes on this matter."

Abby was saddened to learn of the death of her friend, Elizabeth Evelyn Anders, and the details of Andy orphaned at such a young age. Abby was shocked that Elizabeth picked her as his guardian.

Abby read the letter a second time. She looked at Andy and quickly sized him up to be a typical ten-year-old. "Welcome to my home Andy, or I guess I should say our home. Ah, I have an empty room for you up in the attic. It's a bit cramped, but I think it will do very nicely for you. Can you give me a hand setting up this month's Mercyville Ladies Book Club Meeting playbill?"

Andy placed his bag on the porch bench next to the front door and helped Aunt Abby set up her meeting sign. He read this month's selection aloud,

"Volume One, Uncle Tom's Cabin,

Life Among the Lowly.

By Harriet Beecher Stowe."

He thought for a minute. "Who's Harriet? Her name sounds familiar. I think my mom talked about her, and even read some letters she received from Harriet to her and her friends."

"Andy, do you see the picture on the playbill?" He nodded his head yes. "She wrote this book to help free the slaves. Other writers glorify slavery. I am proud to say that she does not do that in her book. Harriet is a famous Hartford, Connecticut abolitionist and she is upstairs right now getting ready to tell us all about the Underground Railroad."

Andy heard the word railroad. "I like riding on the railroad with those great big steam engines and all the chugging and screaming steam. Does she own a steam engine? Do you think she would let me go for a ride on her train?"

Abby realized Andy had no idea what she was talking about, so Abby quickly decided the less she said to Andy about the underground railroad, the safer and better off she would feel.

"I'm sorry. Andy, I gave you the wrong impression. Harriet does not own a railroad. Just like you, she enjoys riding the rails." That seemed to satisfy his natural curiosity.

However, she still worried and felt that she may have said too much to Andy for his young age, especially, with the twelve ladies arriving soon for her book club meeting. She added distractingly, "Andy, thank you for helping me set up the stand. Have you had breakfast?" He shook his head no.

"Good, because I made some fresh molasses walnut muffins and strawberry preserve scones. After you are settled in upstairs, if you promise to play outside all morning, you may have one of each."

The Boy in the Attic

Andy thought it was a grand idea to be allowed outside to play on his first day living here, so naturally, he nodded his head in agreement.

Aunt Abby grinned, "Good for you. Now let us find you a room in the attic where you will be staying. After you unpack, come on down for your muffin and scone, and go play outside. You really don't want to hear a bunch of women chattering to each other for hours. Now do you?"

As Andy climbed the inn's first flight of stairs, he marveled at how wide, smooth, and highly polished the oak banisters was just right for sliding down. The second and third floors only had hand railings and were not suitable for sliding at all.

Abby brought him to a pull-down hatch in the ceiling of the third floor. She examined how short the pull chain was, and inquired of her new charge, "This will never do, Andy. Can you really reach this pull chain? I don't think so. Please try it."

Andy looked around, feeling surrounded by all the purple, lavender flowered wallpaper, and put his carpetbag out of the way by a small hall table. He came back and made his best effort at jumping for the pull-down chain. His efforts were all to no avail, for every time Andy jumped, gravity kept him from reaching it. He missed reaching the pull chain by just the tips of his fingers. "Alright Andy, that's enough jumping for one day. I'll have the handyman fix up a longer pull chain for you. This time I will help you up."

Aunt Abby easily reached up, and as she tugged the pull-down chain, it stuck. The third time, the hatchway popped open with some paint flakes sprinkling down on them, "Oh, I forgot, I had the ceiling repainted, and the hatchway was just plain paint stuck. Now up you go. I'll get a handyman to fix it for you."

Andy scurried up the ladder and was just the right height not to hit his head on the low slanting ceiling. The attic room had a twin bed with a small bureau across from it, and it had a window seat. Andy always wanted a window seat. He plopped his bag on his bed, and a plume of light dust engulfed the room.

He sneezed as he looked out the window. Putting his nose against the window glass, he could see the horse-drawn carriages going by the front of the inn. Soon a carriage with a foul-looking driver pulled up in front of the inn. Andy saw a woman in the carriage argue with the driver, just before she took her daughter's hand and got out of the carriage.

Andy pressed his forehead against the window glass, trying to see if he could see them walk up the sidewalk to the inn's front doors.

The woman was now half dragging her young daughter along with her. You know, the way mothers do when their child does not want to go somewhere. Andy thought the pretty red-haired girl didn't want to visit today. She looked up at him, and she had the prettiest green eyes Andy ever did see. He pressed his face against the window trying to see more, but they stepped onto the porch out of his view. He hollered good and loud, "Aunt Abby, you got guests coming up the sidewalk."

"Thank you. Unpack and make yourself at home. I have to see to my guests. Don't forget your treats when you go out to play."

He hightailed it downstairs. Sliding down the first-floor banister and misjudging the distance, he landed plumb in front of the little red-haired girl, who giggled as he flopped on the floor. Andy grinned, "Hi I'm Andy. Do you want a scone?"

She nodded her head yes and then quickly looking around she whispered, "I'm Angela Fishkill-Katz, can I slide down the banister too?"

First Inaugural Address

Monday, March 4, 1861

In your hands, my dissatisfied fellow-countrymen, and not in mine, is the momentous issue of civil war. The Government will not assail you. You can have no conflict without being yourselves the aggressors. You have no oath registered in heaven to destroy the Government, while I shall have the most solemn one to "preserve, protect, and defend it."

President Abraham Lincoln

CHAPTER ONE

TROUBLE ARRIVES

Since Andy moved into the Mercyville Inn, he overslept every day for the last eight years and today was no exception. He rushed around his room throwing on his clothes. Now late for work at the mayor's office, he half jumped down the attic ceiling ladder and raced down the top two flights of stairs. From the second floor, he slid down the banister to the lobby and launched himself at the front door of the inn.

His Aunt Abby lovingly hollered at him as he flew by her, "Stop right there, young man! You got a note from the mayor this morning."

He almost fell over in mid-stride and came back to her. Smiling, he gave her a polite kiss on her cheek.

"What does it say?" Andy asked his Aunt Abby.

"It says, Andy stop sliding down our banister or you'll break your neck one of these days."

Teasingly, he quickly responded, "I don't think the mayor cares about my neck. Does the note really say that about sliding down the banister?"

Aunt Abby shook her head. "Here take it and find out for yourself. You know how to read. After all, ever since you moved in with me eight years ago, you have read every book I own and some twice. Now get going! You are already late for work."

He grabbed a cookie from the plate on the guest's sideboard, and tore open the envelope:

Andrew, go to Train Station at
6:45 and pick up Captain Olson
bring him to New City Hall.
Honorable Mayor Katz

Andy popped open his gold pocket watch. It was already 6:35. "Hmm, just enough time to pick up the carriage from work. Oh good, I can see Angela when I drop the captain off this morning." Smiling, he stuffed the cookie into his mouth and the note in his pocket.

TROUBLE ARRIVES

Bolting out of the inn, he slammed the front door behind him and dashed down the sidewalk. He almost ran into the bundled up and bonneted members of the book club as they all came up the sidewalk, arriving early on this chilly morning.

The door bounced open. Abby shook her head as she went to close the door, smiling, "I give up. Even after eight years of living here, Andy will never learn how to close a door without slamming it," She was still laughing as she welcomed the book club members.

~~~

The train from Washington D. C. chugged north through the night, arriving in Hartford, Connecticut in the pre-dawn light, and then making a quick stop at the Mercyville Train Station to let off just one passenger, before proceeding northeast onto Providence.

Captain Nickolas Oldstone arrived at the train station to change the future of Mercyville forever. He knew about the long-time allegiances of Mercyville with the south. After all, as the cigar wrapper capital of the Union, the town's loyalty was being questioned because of its close ties with the Richmond slave trade.

As the six forty-five train pulled into the station, Captain Oldstone got up and folded up his copy of a Hartford newspaper.

When he was ready to disembark, he slipped the paper beneath his arm. Anyone could quickly read the
~~~

front-page headlines filled with the news of the rebel's firing on Fort Sumter and the Special Session of Congress calling for war and President Lincoln issuing a call for 75,000 volunteer troops.

The captain tidied up and brushed his slept-in tailored dress uniform and straightened his medals. He had earned his medals proudly during the Mexican-American War of 1846. General Winfield Scott, Old Fuss and Budget, always stressed to him to make sure his medals were always perfectly pinned to his dress jacket, all in a neat row.

Captain Oldstone brought with him none of his staff for this part of his journey. In fact, for security reasons, his arrival in Mercyville was kept a secret. He traveled alone and carried only his carpetbag filled with the paperwork and documentation he needed to accomplish his mission.

As he stepped off the train, he was greeted by the fast-talking mayor's aide, who was already starting to rattle off a deluge of words barely audible over the noise of the busy train depot, "Captain Olson! Captain Olson! Hi, I am Andy Anders. Mayor Katz sent me to pick you up and bring you over to the new city hall. Do you have any luggage?"

"Greetings Andy! I don't have any luggage except for my carpetbag, and my name is pronounced Oldstone and not Olson, and to be more precise, I'm Captain Nickolas Oldstone."

Andy nodded his head in reply as he took the carpetbag from him, "Right this way to our carriage sir."

As they headed down the station platform, the captain inquired, "Andy, before we start off for city hall, does Mercyville have any newspaper offices? I have some printing I need to do."

"Yes, sir! We have two fine papers for you to choose from, either the Mercyville Post or the Mercyville Republican. Let me get you one of each from the Station Master."

Andy ran off before the captain could say another word and he returned with both of them, "Here you go, sir. With the compliments from Mayor Katz."

"Thank you, Andy. Oh! One more thing. I need to know what your true feelings are about the Rebellion. Where do your loyalties lie? I have to know I can trust you. Give it to me straight."

Quite assuredly Andy quickly replied, "Sir, after what I have seen up here in the shade-grown tobacco fields of the Connecticut Valley and the Connecticut River ports, I am definitely an abolitionist."

Andy thought for a moment before continuing, "Since slavery was banned here in 1848, the tobacco growers skirt the law by calling the slaves seasonal help or indentured labor. The slave traders pack the laborers into the holds of old outdated whaling ships like so many whale oil barrels. They transport them from the Manchester Slave

Docks in Richmond by the sea route through Long Island Sound and up the river to the mayor's private docks across from Hartford. It is unfortunate to watch the slave traders unload their half-dead human cargo in our ports."

Sadly, Andy continued, "In the spring, they import them from the south to work and plant the tobacco fields and then send the bulk of them back after they finish planting. In the fall, the tobacco growers bring back the slaves to handpick their wrapper leaves and hang the leafy stalks in the drying barns. They work the slaves from sun up to late in the night. Far too many of them never make it back to the south. On top of that, we are told to look the other way by the more aggressive growers, or else."

Andy sounding a bit confused remarked, "Also, last month the abolitionist Mercyville Republican newspaper office had their windows smashed in by bricks with death threats tied to them. Why just last week someone tried to burn it down. Fortunately, they were scared off by Old Ham, a local night watchman, who gave the perpetrators a rear end full of rock salt." Andy laughingly added, "Both barrels too I might add."

The captain wondered, "Andy did the law catch them?"

"No sir, but I might add that a couple of the mayor's police officers limped very noticeably for a while, and they now prefer to stand and not sit these days." The captain chuckled when he heard this.

"Anyway sir, we now have the Mercyville police force, and the mayor seems to have the Police Chief in his back pocket, so to speak. It seems every time something destructive happens to the newspaper office, the mayor just happens to need the officer on duty to look into something minor elsewhere."

"Has anything harmful been done against the Mercyville Post?" Oldstone questioned.

Andy sighed and said, "No worries over there. Not with the mayor having a half interest in it,"

While Andy talked, the captain briefly looked at the two newspapers that Andy handed him earlier. Neither headline had a single word about the attack on Fort Sumter or the President's Declaration of War. Putting them away, he inquired, "I take it the mayor has an interest in the Mercyville Station Telegraph office?"

"Oh yes, the mayor definitely has a hidden interest in the telegraph office."

The captain asked quizzically, "Andy, how do you know so much about the mayor's business?"

"I do a lot of part-time jobs to make ends meet, and his bookkeeper needs help once in a while. Besides, the mayor is a bit of a loud talker when he is wound up, and his voice tends to echo through the central heating vents. Except when he is planning something underhanded, then you cannot hear him. He has been doing a lot of whispering these days. Something is very wrong here in Mercyville."

Union Captain Oldstone tried to reassure Andy, consoling him, "I assure you that after my visit and business dealings here in Mercyville, things are going to be changing pretty quickly for the better up here, I might add. That is a promise! With the South breaking away, there will be no more slave shipments coming north, and we'll see what can be done to stop the attacks on abolitionists."

Andy sighed, speaking very slowly and clearly, "In that case Captain, if you're really going to take on the mayor, I would not turn my back on him if I were you."

Andy continued, "I may be related to him by a distant cousin who is twice removed on my mother's side of our family, but he is no friend of mine. They say blood is thicker than water, but with him, it is not true. I know for sure he sold his soul to the southern slave traders a long time ago. That's how he could afford to build that grand palace he calls a city hall and afford his lifestyle."

Quizzically, Captain Oldstone inquired, "I'm not surprised. How does he treat you and others who work for him?"

Disgusted, Andy paused, "Excuse me for saying so, but he pays us late and docks our pay almost every day for some of the most ridiculous reasons.

"What bothers me most though is, how shall I put it, I will just say it as I see it, sir. He imported three Irish blacksmiths to build the city halls ironwork decorations and two Italian glassmakers to make his precious stained-glass windows for the new Mercyville City Hall. Last week when they demanded their backpay and refused to continue working until they got what was owed to them, he claimed they overcharged him and were cheating him."

Oldstone now curious, "What happened next?"

"The next day they didn't show up for work. First, Mayor Katz claimed he fired them, but now he claims he paid them to catch a ship back to Ireland and Italy."

The captain questioned Andy, "You're sure they didn't go back?"

"Sir, no one goes back to Ireland or Italy once they come to America. They all told me there would be no reason to go back because their families were starving there. They were all planning to bring their families over, as soon as they earned enough money to pay for the transatlantic ticket fares.

"I knew these men, sir. They were good men. They would not run out on finishing the last window and iron florets on the front entranceway of the City Hall. If they were paid their back wages, the work would be done, and they would have said goodbye."

The captain mulled this over, "Andy, you're positive and not just letting off steam?"

Andy took a deep breath, "Yes sir, I'm sure. As I mentioned earlier, the mayor does not know I do bookkeeping part-time. I make many of the entries in the ledgers for the bookkeeper. He pays me under the table.

"I found out the mayor keeps a second set of books, but I have not found them yet. Nowhere in any of the books do the Irishmen show up. I am sure they were never paid, nor any money disbursed for their travel anywhere. However, I noticed an entry in the books I keep, a large payment to a slave trader for removing some spoiled cargo the night they disappeared."

Oldstone was speechless with rage over their disappearance and this revelation. Andy handled the horse reins skillfully as they made their way by carriage to the newly constructed city hall.

As they continued on their way there, Andy apologized, "Sorry about mispronouncing your name Captain Oldstone, but it was misspelled on the note the mayor gave me to pick you up. We got that all straightened out, right captain?"

Even though he was upset over the missing men, the captain chuckled and nodded in agreement. Half-aloud and half-thinking to himself, "Andy, have you considered volunteering and helping to put down this Rebellion?"

Andy did not even hesitate as his words quickly flowed, "If war breaks out, I just might. I'm eighteen, and the thought has crossed my mind. Sir, I do not know what

I would be good for. I have never been in a fistfight or used a sword or bayonet, but I did a bit of wrestling and am a fair shot with a rifle on a good calm day. I play second base on the Mercyville Cherubs baseball team, haven't hit a home run yet. I really don't know what you'd do with me."

Oldstone thoughtfully replied, "Andy, you have more opportunities than you know. I would like to talk to you about them after I meet with the mayor. For now, let's not mention our discussions to anyone?"

Andy quickly nodded in agreement, as he pointed at the new city hall up ahead, "We're almost there, sir."

Moments later Andy pulled up on the reins, stopping the horse-drawn carriage. He climbed off and flipped the end of the reins around a rather ornately designed hitching post. The captain looked at it oddly, as if asking what the dickens was on top of it. Andy noticed his look, and leaned over to him and whispered in confidence, "It's a cherub's face and wings. Ah, before I forget to mention it, the mayor prefers to be addressed as the honorable Mayor Katz, and he loves cherubs as you are about to discover in our new city hall."

"Honorable Mayor Katz and cherubs, huh?" The captain took in a deep breath, "Okay, let's head in. I've got to see this place."

The captain stepped off the carriage, and he could not help admiring the stately imposing building façade still under construction. He noticed the unfinished iron gates and almost completed stained glass windows. "I knew Mercyville was rich and famous from its thread mills and tobacco wrapper plantations, but not this wealthy and ostentatious."

On hearing this, Andy pretended small-town pride, grinning ear to ear, puffed up his chest and replied good and loud so the mayor would hear him, "Yes sir, our Most Honorable Mayor Aloysius T. Katz has been most generous to us since his election."

Andy's words echoed in the marble hall entryway. "Our community has been blessed to have such a wise businessman as our leader, Mayor Aloysius T. Katz. His building plans are par excellence if I dare say so myself."

Watching the young man boast gave Captain Oldstone the feeling that the honorable Mayor Aloysius T. Katz was truly a man of conceit and highly questionable business practices. Good and loud he asked, as if impressed, "So there is a lot of money to be made here by an adventurous businessman, huh Andy?"

Andy was glad the captain caught onto what he was doing, "Oh yes sir, we are truly a booming business community where everyone who is anyone deserves to profit from his efforts. Right this way sir, the Honorable Mayor's office is straight up the atrium stairs."

Andy's words were the exact words the captain wanted to hear about Mercyville, but he was more interested in hearing those exact words coming from the mayor himself. The captain headed up the granite steps of the brand new, but still unfinished, Mercyville City Hall.

Once they were through the gates and past the unfinished stained-glass doors, they stepped into a marbled atrium facing an over-built, wide-flowing marble staircase covered in cherubs. It was right across from the main entranceway they had just stepped through. The captain realized, he was right about Katz building the new city hall to impress others, but he wondered whom? It was by far too large a building for Mercyville. It might be needed in a hundred or more years, but not anytime sooner.

Andy was right too. Everywhere the captain looked were cherubs staring back at him. Some smiled or laughed, or what appeared to be singing. How very odd the captain thought.

Looking up at the top of the staircase, they could see the Mayor standing there. He was impeccably suited for the day and wearing a broad black cummerbund around his potbelly. He reminded Oldstone of a foreign dignitary or a potentate beckoning him up the stairs to his doom.

"Come on up, Captain Oldstone. The air is rarified up here in anticipation of a successful business deal between us. Isn't my Mercyville City Hall magnificent? Don't you just love those winged cherubs on the corners and along the top molding? I paid a fortune for them and what about my portrait over the reception area. Magnificent isn't it?"

Chapter One

"I assure you, your Honor, I have never seen another building such as this building outside of Washington D.C. In fact, it probably outshines most buildings in the District and in the other towns, which I have entered on my long journey to get here. I'll be right up." As Oldstone spoke, he could see that the mayor was truly beside himself in anticipation of his arrival. The mayor's pupils dilated with the excitement of bringing more money to Mercyville or was it just for himself.

Turning to Andy, the captain whispered only loud enough to be heard by Andy, "Thank you for filling me in on what is really going on here and carrying my bag this far for me. I have to take it the rest of the way upstairs, alone. Oh, one more thing just between you and me. After this meeting, I need to talk to you about something of great importance to you."

Andy winked surreptitiously and handed the carpetbag over to him. "Good luck sir."

As the captain began his climb up to the mayor's office, Andy headed over to talk to Angela the red-head receptionist, behind the oak welcome desk.

Andy was sweet on Angela, but with her being Mayor Katz's stepdaughter, they did not get many opportunities to talk. Except when Mayor Katz closed his office door, of course. They would sneak off for lunch in the garden or park, where the mayor never strolled. Otherwise, they always winked or very discretely smooched at each other from a distance. They carried on behind the mayor's back with knowing little loving smiles.

Fortunately for Andy and Angela, the mayor never noticed their love for one another because all he ever cared about was power and money. Katz married Angela's mother for her money. Her death was just a matter of monetary convenience to him.

Katz was overly proud and downright arrogant about being a self-made land baron. He would stop at nothing to get a controlling interest in anything local, and he did as he pleased, no matter who got hurt.

According to local gossip, Katz was suspected of having his fingers in every business in town. In fact, his reach did grab something from almost every business including the Mercyville Post, which was owned by the Falsemouth family and seemed to be wrapped around his little finger.

However, Katz was still irked that he could not get rid of the abolitionist Republican newspaper. He despised both that newspaper and the inn because they believed in and supported abolition. Katz really despised the Quakers, and all abolitionists, because in the 1840s they cost his family their slaves when Connecticut outlawed slavery.

Andy and Angela often overheard Katz intimidating people by taunting them how his father taught him to use legal loopholes to get what he wanted. They would cringe whenever he said, "All you do is pay off the right judges and have the police chief in your back pocket, and you can get away with murder."

CHAPTER TWO

UNCONDITIONAL SURRENDER

Mayor Katz heard a dry cough behind his back. Looking over his shoulder, he spotted Francis Falsemouth of the Post newspaper leaning against the wall. Falsemouth was obstructing the view of the mayor's new brass plaque, Katz unforgivingly demanded. "What are you still doing here?"

The young man faking concern, snidely replied, "Why your honor, did you forget that you invited me over to record this momentous occasion for prosperity?"

In no mood to have his victory over the captain ruined by this pipsqueak, the mayor lowered his voice and meanly hissed back at Falsemouth, "Get out! Once I get what I want from the captain, I'll give you my headline, and your father had better get it right word for word this time. Now get out and use the back stairs." The mayor regained his grin as he turned back to see how much the captain was out of breath from climbing the steps.

Captain Oldstone made his way up the thirty-nine marble steps of the Mercyville City Hall. With every step he took, he passed another cherub intertwined in the grape vines embossed all over the banisters, newels and hand railings.

Teasingly, the mayor inquired, "Tell me Captain Oldstone the marble steps are marvelously carved, aren't they? Tell me, have you ever met the man Elisha Otis?"

The captain, being a little over halfway up the flight of stairs, stopped and stared up at the self-important mayor, "Yes they are marvelously carved. No, I do not know the man. Did he carve all these cherubs?"

Katz chuckled, "No captain, Otis didn't carve any of them, he is a far too important man to do that because he is the future. I met him at the 1854 New York World's Fair. He is a very important successful businessperson, you might say that he is an inspiration to me. Sadly, he passed away on the 8th of this month, so I am wearing this black cummerbund and armband in memory of him until the end of the month."

The captain continued up the flight of stairs reaching almost the top. "I'm very sorry to hear of your loss. My condolences to you."

Mayor Katz replied, "I admired Elisha Otis, not just because he saw a need for a new invention, but because he acted on it and boldly profited from it. You see, businessmen have to act swiftly or be left behind these days."

As the mayor spoke, the captain continued his climb, thinking how long winded the mayor was.

When the captain reached the top, he went to shake the mayor's hand. Just as the captain expected, the mayor stepped forward and firmly grasped the captain's hand and started squeezing it as hard as he could. But to the mayor's surprise, the captain's hand was hard as a rock. Very quickly, the mayor felt the hard, cold squeeze of the captain's hand crushing his grip. The mayor catching his breath, sputtered, "Well, you definitely have a firm grip, Captain. You would make an admirable businessman and partner."

Captain Oldstone released the mayor's hand, and chose his words very carefully, "Yes, the reality is that a cavalry officer has to have a firm grasp on the reins or lose control of his steed."

The captain noticed as soon as he said those words, the mayor's smile weakened just a little bit.

The glint returned to the mayor's eyes as he continued about Otis, "Come over here Captain, and you will see the modern marvel created by Elisa Otis here in our city hall. Why even the White House and Capitol building in Washington D. C. does not have an elevator, but we do have an elevator all because of me. Captain, I will give you the future."

With the wave of his arm, the mayor pointed to the elevator doors on their left, across from his office. "Come over here captain and take a good look at my elevator. The elevator company even installed a commemorative brass plaque. Come over here and be the first member of the public to read it."

Captain Oldstone decided to humor the mayor and stepped over to read the plaque's inscription. The small six-inch square brass plaque embossed with cherubs read:

April 15, 1861

This Mercyville City Hall Elevator

Is the first elevator to be installed in a

Southern New England City Hall

for the Progressive and Honorable

Mayor Aloysius Thaddeus Katz

"Captain, you are now part of my living history to this community, for you are the first member of the public to see the first elevator in a City Hall in all of Connecticut and Southern New England. Now isn't that something special about Mercyville? Doesn't that just scream progress and confidence in Mercyville to you? We are the most progressive New Englanders in Mercyville, and you should not have any doubts about building your Union Army camp in Mercyville, Connecticut. Come into my office and let's cut a deal and get that army base built here in Mercyville."

Oldstone stepped into the mayor's office expecting to be surrounded by cherubs everywhere. Instead, the walls and moldings were immaculately smooth without a single cherub or carving on them. Even more so the conference table, Katz's desk, and bookshelves were empty, "Please excuse my office. We haven't moved everything over from the old town hall yet. It will be a couple of more days before we complete our move over here. Perhaps you would rather postpone our meeting until all the town land records have arrived?"

Rather bluntly the mayor heard just one word from his guest, "Nope."

The mayor sighed and closed his office door and took his seat behind his large cherry wood desk, "Please captain take a seat and let's cut a deal."

"Mayor, I have all the records I need for my site selection and land purchases to be made by the US Government. If I might ask, where is the old town hall?"

The mayor tried to hide his surprise behind a wide grin, "It's just an old run-down building on the north side across from the train station. It's of no importance to our discussions. It is the past and not the future. You said land purchases. I thought with all the talk of a short war to put down the Rebellion that you would prefer to rent the land." He gave the captain a small sly wink.

"No, I am here to purchase, not rent tobacco fields, so shall we get started?" Captain Oldstone thought quizzically for a moment, "Aren't you going to bring in the Town Council or elders to join our meeting?"

Acting offended, his honor the mayor digressed, "Nonsense, over one hundred years ago my family relocated up here from Dixie and founded Mercyville. I am the one in charge, and I am going to bring progress and prosperity here. I will bring your encampment here to Mercyville. My vote overrides everyone else's vote on the council. Besides, they are always indecisive and just hold things up. I want progress for Mercyville in these changing times, sir. I think you and I can come to a much better decision, and much quicker decision, together. I believe your time is of the utmost importance to you? Don't you agree?"

The only thing Captain Oldstone agreed on was the long-windedness of Mayor Katz. "Yes Mayor, my time is of importance to me. However, the community needs to understand why we are here and what I expect of them."

Mayor Katz sighed deeply, "Alright, that is a good point. As the head of the town council, I am the one you must negotiate with. How much land, materials, supplies, and day labor will you need to procure, rent or purchase from us?"

"To start with I brought copies of the Connecticut survey maps and state records from 1860 for Mercyville and the other locales we are contacting. I need to go over the Mercyville records with you. Can we move to the conference table and I will spread the Mercyville map out for you?"

Mayor Katz replied offendedly, "I'm not aware of any 1860 survey of our land here. Let me see those so-called state maps you brought."

The captain removed the maps from his carpetbag and spread the Mercyville map out on the table, "See right here is the town boundaries of Mercyville, as you can see the rail line cuts through the northern portion of your town along here. As you can see this tobacco farm borders on the rail right of way." Oldstone paused, waiting for a reaction from Katz, but none came.

Oldstone continued talking, "To the north of the train station and rail right of way is this tobacco farm. It's 1200 acres."

Katz rudely interrupted him, "It's a tobacco plantation owned by my brother. This property has been in my family for over 100 years, ever since my ancestors first moved here from our homeland in Dixie."

The captain insisted, "Mayor, these flat fields are exactly what my engineers say we need. This tobacco plantation is the site I want to see the first thing tomorrow morning."

The mayor's jaw dropped open, "That's out of the question! We just planted those tobacco crops, and it is a sizable investment. You are asking me to give up growing our tobacco wrappers for our cigar business, for what? So, you can destroy prime tobacco land, for what your stupid parade ground to march around on?"

Katz, trying to bully this Yankee captain into submission, nastily continued, "Captain, that land will be tied up for the rest of the year. However, over here on the south side of town is the land you should be looking at for your base. It is over two thousand acres of undeveloped woodland. We can have it cleared in three or four months for the right price. The earliest your troops could move in there would be near the end of August or early September."

The captain thought for a few moments, "That's not acceptable. There is no immediate rail access to that area. We are only interested in what we can immediately obtain and occupy for our Union Army to put down this Rebellion. Your tobacco plantation on the north side of the train station and the rail right of way is perfect for our needs."

Katz replied over-confidently still pushing the wooded terrain, "Well, if you pay us enough then we will gladly build you a rail spur to the east over here between these two hills. Of course, you do realize it will all depend on how generous your labor contracts are. You should still be able to relocate your troops there by the end of September."

Oldstone anticipated this problem with Katz, "I don't think you understand Mister Katz. We need the land now. Our troops will be arriving any day and not in three to six months' time. I do have authorization from the Federal Government, and permission to proceed from your State of Connecticut's governor. I brought with me a copy of the Governor's letter. It gives me carte blanche powers in this matter. Do you want to see it?"

Indignantly, the mayor replied, "That is absurd sir! I am the local authority here, and you need my permission as well to make this work. Now take the land in the south, or take nothing at all and lead your troops elsewhere."

The captain sternly replied, "I will take what we need and provide fair compensation to the landowners."

"Oh really! And how much would that be?" The mayor demanded to know.

Oldstone reached into his carpetbag and removed a packet of bundled papers marked 'Mercyville.' Shuffling through the papers, he finally found the records he was looking for, "Unless you lied to the state's Office of the Comptroller about the value and ownership of your family land sales and transfers."

He paused as he checked the numbers on the document, "Here is a copy of the land values you registered with the state for the tobacco plantation north of town that is in question."

Unconditional Surrender

Captain Oldstone handed the Mercyville registered land records and pricing papers over to Mayor Katz to read and waited for the mayor's reaction.

It did not take long before Katz behaved like a spoiled two-year-old. At first, he yelled and screamed, and finally tried to bully the captain into relenting to him.

Holding firm, Oldstone looked man to man into Katz's eyes, "Here are the facts of life, Mister Katz. Not you, not a member of your family, not your organization, not a town member, not a hired gun will interfere with my military business here. If even one person acts against us, you will be held personally responsible and charged with treason. We know all about your dealings with the slave traders, that you are laundering money for the rebels, and that you own the tobacco plantation and not your brother. Do I make myself clear, Mister Katz?"

Dejectedly, Katz plopped down on the edge of his desk to think about his next move against this carpet-bagging Yankee. Infuriated, he swore under his breath to kill Oldstone or die trying.

"Mister Katz." He was unresponsive, so the captain raised his voice even more, "Mayor Katz! Do what is right for your community and cooperate with us. That way Mercyville will profit from the Union Army, instead of just you, this is not a request. It is a demand."

Captain Oldstone shuffled through the papers again and took out a form, "Here, read this quick claim and sign your tobacco plantation over to the U. S. Government and I will be on my way. Oh, one other thing, if you stay south of the rail line, you and I will never need to do business again."

Desperately, thinking quickly, Katz muttered, "I also need my brother's signature."

"No, you don't." Oldstone handed Katz a copy of the year-old land registration filed with the state. "You see Katz, you forgot, it became public knowledge when your brother transferred ownership one hundred percent over to you. See right there is your signature and his."

Katz Screamed, "You Dirty Dog! May you die and rot in those fields for a hundred years!"

Ignoring the mayor's curse, "As soon as you sign it, I'll be able to transfer the money to your bank account in Hartford."

Shocked, Katz stuttered, "You even know about my bank accounts in Hartford?"

Wryly, the captain continued, "And the bank accounts in Richmond, Atlanta and New Orleans for your profits from the slave trade and illegal cotton smuggling. Oh, and we discovered the one in London, which you use for the money laundering."

The captain remembered about the old town hall, "Oh Katz, by chance that old rundown town hall wouldn't happen to be on the tobacco plantation, would it? If so, I claim it as public domain property. I am sure it will make a nice staff headquarters. Make sure you have your stuff out tomorrow, or my troops will clean it out for you. I am sure you have personal records or even dirty laundry you do not want to air in public. I doubt if I would be able to stop any acts of vengeance by any of my troopers, who discovered your dirty little secrets."

The mayor's face turned red as a beet, but he just clenched his fists and sat there on the edge of his rosewood desk vowing vengeance against this Yankee captain and the Union.

Seeing the look on Katz's face, "Oh, shall I continue Mayor Katz? Maybe you should quit while you're still ahead and consider yourself lucky. You see, if it were up to me, I would put you up against a wall without a blindfold and have you shot for treason. It's a shame you are not in the military, or martial law is not in effect yet. Therefore, I highly encourage you to sign the paperwork so I can reimburse you and I can get going. After all, I have engineers, surveyors, and troops arriving tomorrow, if not sooner."

From the reception area, Andy and Angela the receptionist heard raised voices coming from the mayor's office on the second floor. With the mayor's door shut, Angela and Andy could not make out what all the screaming by the mayor was about, but he sounded the same as a wounded animal caught in a nasty bear trap would sound.

With green eyes as wide as saucers, Angela stared fearfully at Andy, "With the way the mayor is shouting at him, do you think he is going to kill him? Or do you think they're going to kill each other?"

Andy laughed, "If I had any money to bet on the outcome, I'd say Captain Oldstone has the upper hand due to his military experience during the Mexican War."

Angela giggled at the thought of Mayor Katz getting his comeuppance at the hands of a Union officer. "Andy, I think you're right, but I would not mind it at all if the captain threw the mayor out his office window. He deserves it with the way he treats us as if he owns us."

Now it was Andy's turn to laugh. Suddenly it went all quiet upstairs in the mayor's office.

Angela asked, "Do you think one of them is dead?"

"I don't know. Let's see who comes out first," whispered Andy. "And we'll declare him the winner."

Angela giggled, again, "Andy, you're so funny, that's why I love you."

As Andy went to kiss her, he watched her bright green eyes roll up toward the mayor's office. She did not hear any more screaming and figured the captain reached a verdict, "Shh, I think I hear someone coming out alive. Let's see who won." She giggled as Andy pulled back from a lost kiss.

As she looked up the staircase, Andy quickly snuck a kiss on her rosy cheek. She blushed and giggled. While he had the chance, he whispered in her ear, "See you tonight in the garden behind the old town hall, like last night." She grinned and nodded yes.

Almost immediately, the mayor's door opened, and out strode Captain Oldstone. He did not appear any worse for wear or tear. However, following him out, Mayor Katz no longer seemed to be as pompous as when the captain first arrived.

However, the mayor's face was now a solid bright-red as red as the angry red planet Mars. From the look on his face, they could easily see that the mayor could just barely contain his anger. He definitely had gotten his comeuppance from the captain.

Andy grinned as the captain descended the grand flight of marble stairs. The mayor seeing the look on Angela and Andy's faces sharply and angrily screamed out, "Andrew, I saw that grin! You're fired! Get out and stay away from my step-daughter, or you won't live to see tomorrow." He stormed back into his office slamming the door behind him.

Andy turned towards Angela, "Tonight at nine, right?" Angela cleared her throat and with lover's stars in her eyes grinned in anticipation.

Captain Oldstone ordered, "Come along Andy. Now that your unemployed, I have a real man's job to offer you as a corporal. Kiss your girl goodbye and follow me." Of course, this was Andy's first order, and he definitely obeyed it before following the captain out of the Mercyville City Hall.

As Andy came outside, he noticed two things: first, Francis Falsemouth and two of his disreputable buddies leaning against the building across the street, and second the captain checking the time on his pocket watch.

"Andy, even though it is a bit premature to call you corporal, take me back to the Mercyville Train Station, as quickly as possible. I am running a few minutes late, and I have a swarm of official dispatches to send out and some very official business to conduct with the telegrapher."

Without another word said, Andy turned the carriage around. From the mayor's office window, Andy heard the mayor bellow, "Falsemouth!"

Andy saw Falsemouth race up the city hall steps two at a time, while his buddies remained across the street. Andy asked the captain, "What's this about making me a corporal, sir?"

"Andy, the first half of my orders are to secure the train station, railway line, and plantation for the Union Army. I can truthfully say I accomplished that in the mayor's office this morning. The other half of my orders are to enlist as many able-bodied recruits from Mercyville and its environs for the Union Army. By the way, congratulations on volunteering."

Andy busily handled the carriage reins, guiding the horses around the potholes in the dirt street while listening intently, "But why me? Why make me a corporal?"

"Andrew, whether you know it or not, you know more about what is going on in Mercyville and who to contact to get things done fast. Am I right?"

"Yes, sir."

"Good, I'd be worried if you said no." The captain added, "I have the authority to grant field promotions, and as soon as we get to the train station, we will sign you up as a private. And then when Sergeant Palgrave says you're ready, I'll field promote you to corporal.

"Excuse me, but earlier you clearly said, 'we,' but you arrived alone, didn't you?" He asked the captain somewhat puzzled.

"Andy, sometimes you have to keep secrets until the right moment. I have not been completely honest with you. I have more troops arriving today to set up a bivouac on the tobacco plantation grounds, and truthfully, when this Rebellion started, I lost my best lieutenant, who was my adjutant officer. Yesterday he sent me a telegram resigning. In it, he said he was joining up with the Virginia Militia to defend his state and not our country."

"Wow Captain, what a turncoat! You have my undying loyalty."

"Good, but I would rather have you be loyal to your country and not the man. However, I accept your pledge to me. I think you will make fine officer material and earn the rank of lieutenant soon enough."

The captain thinking aloud said, "Sergeant Palgrave has the paperwork. He will make it all official, and even witness your enlistment papers and get you started on earning your promotions."

Andy swerved to miss a pothole. "One last thing sir. Won't the men be upset with you promoting me?" He asked questioningly.

"Not at all Andy. We are bringing on board new troops, and we need new officers to replace all those who graduated from West Point and deserted to the rebel cause. We are in desperate need of new officers, and the door is wide open for bright promotable young volunteers. Besides, I need an adjutant officer with your bookkeeping skills and knowledge of Mercyville. You could easily handle the administrative camp duties for me."

The captain added, "The last time there were any field promotions was during the war with Mexico, and we won it with almost all recruits, including myself.

"In fact, it was during the Vera Cruz Campaign, I inadvertently earned my first promotion and got the nickname 'Old Nick.' I wasn't much older than you are now. Come to think of it, the enlisted men refer to me with pride as 'Old Nick' behind my back.

"Nowadays the Generals call me it in an endearing and non-frustrating way. Whenever they need something special finished early, just in time, or to clean up someone else's mess up, every one of them asks for my help."

The captain laughingly stated, "At first I was offended by my nickname, but I discovered how useful it became when issuing orders to my staff, troops, and recruits." Andy could not help but laugh too.

"Andy! Quick! Pull up!" Excitedly, the captain almost jumped out of the carriage while Andy was reining in his horses. "Did we just pass the Mercyville Republican Newspaper office back there? Quick Andy, is it?"

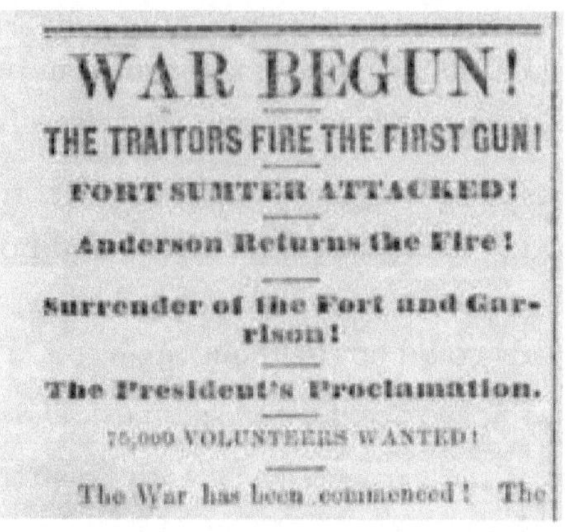

THE RIGHTEOUS CAUSE

Andy looked back over his shoulder at the Mercyville Republican newspaper office, "Yes sir, that's the Republican's office. As I said before, we only have two newspapers in town the Mercyville Post and the Mercyville Republican."

Taking out his carpetbag, Nick pulled out his copy of the Washington newspaper he brought on the train trip north to New England. "Andy, tell me truthfully. Have either of the Mercyville newspapers printed any of these headlines?"

Andy's eyes got as big as saucers as he read aloud the headlines of the Washington newspaper:

The War Begun!
Traitors Fire the First Gun!
Fort Sumter Attacked!
President's Proclamation
75,000 Volunteers Wanted!

"No sir, I have not read about the Fort Sumter disaster in either of our newspapers. Is it true?"

Ignoring Andy's question, Nick had an urgent question of his own, "Andy, the sign in the window states that the editor and owner is one Haywood Worthington. Does everyone call him Woody? Quick lad, tell me if it's true."

"Yes sir, he bought the Mercyville Times a few years ago and renamed it the Re...."

Before Andy could finish his sentence, the captain moved, as fast as a squirrel, and was already out of the carriage. With his newspaper in hand, he headed toward the Mercyville Republican Newspaper office.

Rapidly, he stepped out of the bright sun and into the shade of the Mercyville Republican Newspaper Office. He found himself standing in front of a tall counter covered with small piles of the day's print edition. Behind the office-counter was Woody, a tall, slim New Englander helping his apprentice Charlie Stanhope operate a somewhat noisy, clanking, old newspaper press - the kind of printing press where the operator could quickly lose a finger or two between the smashing ink plates if he weren't careful.

The captain mischievously grinned as he quietly rearranged the piles of newspapers into one pile in front of him, to hide his face behind. He also took off his hat. Otherwise, it would have been a sure give-a-way.

Holding up a piece of paper, as high up as he could, Nick shook it in the air as if it were a bill of sale, and he proceeded to wave it at the busy printer. In a loud and clear fake southern accent, he shouted, "Excuse me! Sir, how much to place an ad to sell a dozen virgin slave girls. I just got back with them from Richmond, and they are ripe for the …."

Before Nick could finish his vulgar and obnoxious joke, the printer grabbed the press handle, turned and launched himself over the countertop to attack Nick. He collided with the pile of papers scattering them onto the floor as he tried to hit Nick with the handle of the press.

Fortunately, Nick was faster and sidestepped him, and pulled him the rest of the way over the countertop onto the wood chip covered floor. Nick pinned him down with a wrestling hold, and yelled, "Woody! Is that any way to greet an old friend?"

Still pinned down Woody half choking exclaimed the best he could, "Nick! You, old war dog! Whatever possessed you to come here, to Mercyville? Why I almost killed you."

Nick was beside himself with laughter, "It's okay Woody, I forgive you." They helped each other up while brushing wood chips off.

"Sorry Woody, I just couldn't help myself. As soon as I realized it was you running this newspaper, I just had to come in. I have some paying business for you."

Doubting Nick's veracity Woody complained, "Yeah, I'll bet you do. What's it going to cost me? Another printing press and wagon load of trouble like when President Pierce sent you to Kansas? I lost everything in Lawrence and almost got killed!"

"Oh yeah, I forgot about that printing press, but you can't complain. You came out with all your body parts, didn't you?" Nick chuckled as Woody looked askance at him.

Then Nick poked Woody with the Washington paper, "No seriously, take a look at this."

Woody grabbed the paper and quickly scanned it, "This happened yesterday! How come the telegrapher hasn't told me or the Post about the Union declaring war on the rebels and the call for volunteers?"

The figure of a young man stepping through the doorway answered, "Because Mayor Katz has the telegrapher in his back pocket and doesn't want anybody to know just yet. Not until he has profited from it first."

Woody looked suspiciously at Andy, "You're Abby's nephew and Mayor Katz's aide, the one who does his books, right?"

Andy, starting to nod affirmatively, was taken back a bit, "How did you know I help with the books?"

Woody laughed, "The bookkeeper does my books too, and has been trying to get me to hire you because he can't read my writing."

Andy thought for a moment, "I don't think I will be able to do your books for a while, but after the Rebellion is put down, we can talk. Right now, I have a much better offer from the captain. Besides, I'm trying to get away from Mayor Katz and his schemes to make himself richer at our expense."

The captain sighed, "Andy raises a good point about Mayor Katz. He's not to be trusted. After my meeting with him, I would say he is definitely behind the nefarious goings on in Mercyville. I appreciated your letter about him, and I was able to act and uncover most of his traitorous dealings, but still, need something more before I can stop him cold."

Woody chimed in, "I have been trying for months to find out the mayor's plans. However, no one in Mercyville seems to know, and if they do, they are keeping it under wraps. He has intimidated most town residents and blackmailed even more to join him. I just wish I had something to print to help nail him today."

The captain mischievously suggested, "For a starter, you have a printing press and the scoop about Fort Sumter and the complete Declaration of War on page three in your hands, which has already been written for you. So why not put out a special edition and tell everyone in Mercyville."

Nick picked up and proceeded to brush some wood chips off his hat, "Besides, if you don't, then who would I pay to place this advertisement on your Front Page about raising an army of seventy-five thousand volunteers?"

Nick handed his half-page Union advertisement over to Woody for printing. "Woody! Remember, I said paid advertisement!"

The captain started piling gold coins on the countertop, "Ah Woody, you can say stop anytime. I know this is more than enough."

Woody just stood there laughing as the coins clunked onto the countertop. Woody quickly scooped them up and headed over to set the type for his special edition. "Nick, I sure could use another hand over here setting this here type. Care to join in the fun?"

"Sorry Woody, I have to get to the train station and have a few words with the station master and telegrapher about not passing on important Union announcements and national news. Something tells me there are going to be big changes coming to Mercyville in the next few days.

Especially with the new transport depot and camp, we are building."

Woody stopped setting type and raised an eyebrow while enquiring, "Do I hear another story coming my way? It is good to see you. Nick, we need to catch up on old times, but for now, suit yourself, be the captain instead of Old Nick, and take care of Union business first." Woody went back to his typesetting and removed Garrison's front-page article and replacing it with Nicks paid Union Army advertisement.

Nick smiled, "Today we're setting up the brand-new Camp Mercyville on the north side of the station. Stop by in a day or two when this madhouse quiets down, alright?"

Woody nodded his head, far too busy to be distracted from setting type.

As they headed out of the newspaper office, the captain brushed the last few wood chips off his uniform and slapped his hat against his leg to get rid of the last of the wood chip dust.

Getting back on the carriage, "Come on Andy let's get to the train station. I'm seriously behind schedule, but it was worth seeing Woody again."

As Andy climbed up on the carriage driver's seat, he noticed Falsemouth's two buddies a bit out of breath hurrying into the Bull's Run Tavern across the street.

In a good mood, Nick continued telling Andy, "Sergeant Thackeray Palgrave ungraciously issued me my nickname the first time we met in Vera Cruz, and it's stuck ever since. I've given him his special nickname too. I call him 'Digger.'"

Nick added, "I have been so blessed to have one of the most ornery, relentless, not so by the book sergeants in the Union Army, who can get things done while watching my back."

Nick thinking out loud said, "Digger is like an old bloodhound, forever howling at my heels whenever I misstep. I swear he even growls at me whenever I step off the straight and narrow pathway."

Nick finished up by giving Andy some good advice, "Andrew, you will not meet a truer soldier in the Union Army. So, when you meet him, say, 'Yes sir, Sergeant Palgrave,' or 'No sir, Sergeant Palgrave.' This way we will have you on his good side in no time at all. Together with his help, you will move up in my chain of command."

As Andy and Captain Oldstone arrived at the Mercyville Station, they saw a sea of disheveled blue-uniformed soldiers waiting on the platform. They could hear someone shouting, "Old Nick's arrived! Line up right to left, you bunch of dog-eared rascals!"

Andy's mouth dropped open at the sight of all the disheveled soldiers hustling to line up.

"Andy! Close your mouth! It's not polite to gawk at Union soldiers because the older troopers do not like it and consider it not just bad luck, but rude. As for the young troopers, they will pick a fight with you as fast as they would ask a pretty girl to dance. Now let's go greet my troops!"

On their arrival at Mercyville station platform, a rather large Sergeant suddenly parted the sea of soldiers and stepped out in front of the carriage. He took the horse reins and called out, "Ah-ten! Hut!" All the soldiers snapped to attention facing Captain Nickolas Oldstone. Miraculously, they stood orderly and in perfect rows. Not one button was unbuttoned, or collar crumpled or cap askew.

Digger did not have to turn around to know this, for if one man were not orderly and perfectly aligned, Digger would smell their fear in the air, and all would suffer for that insult to the captain.

The captain stepped onto the platform as Digger sharply raised his arm to salute. All soldiers followed him in near perfect salutes to Captain Nickolas Oldstone. Proudly the captain saluted them back, and he ever so slightly nodded his head to Digger, who loudly proclaimed, "At Ease." Like a well-oiled machine, they relaxed their stance but remained standing in their perfect formation awaiting orders.

"Welcome to Mercyville. I shall be brief. It is with great honor being back with you today.

"It is getting late in the day. We need the encampment set up now, or we will all be sleeping under the cold April stars, or in the rain tonight."

Holding up the quick deed, he continued in a clear, firm voice, "This entire tobacco plantation from this station platform all the way up to the northern border of Mercyville by the red sandstone cliffs, belongs to us. Our camp includes the entire north side of the railway which is now Union Army property. You all know your place and have your assignments. Thank you for coming to Mercyville in our country's time of need. Digger, there will soon be plenty of new young recruits for you to whip into shape for the coming dark times."

Digger turned toward the men, "Let's hear three cheers for Old Nick!"

The troop's response was swift and uniform, "Hurrah! Hurrah! Hurrah for Old Nick!"

Digger loudly ordered all within earshot, "Dismissed! Now get to work! You have your orders! And don't forget to report back on your status or you'll see my ugly face haunting you until you're done." Turning away from them, he noticed Andy for the first time standing there, "And who are you supposed to be?"

Before Andy could respond, Nick interjected with a grin. "Digger, it's not who he is? It is who do you think he will become?"

Teasingly, Digger faked thinking by rubbing his chin and pulling on his scruffy looking grey beard, "Hmm, this has to be one of your real twisted conundrums. Wait, let me guess. I got it! He is going to be your new lieutenant to replace that cowardly dog of a traitor who ran off to the rebels. Did I guess right?"

Smiling confidently the captain gave the thumb up, "You know me pretty well Digger. Allow me to introduce Master Andrew Anders, soon to be Private Anders with your approval of course.

Andrew, meet my favorite Sergeant in the whole Union Army, Sergeant Thackeray Palgrave. The man who quite literally whipped me into shape and taught me how to soldier during the Mexican-American War."

While continuing to grin Nick added, "I expect him to pay you the same disrespect and uncourteous treatment, which I so richly deserved. And I expect Sergeant Palgrave to run you ragged until you've earned your promotions and are turned over to me." The sergeant's chest puffed up, as a father's chest would, with genuine pride in how Nick turned out.

"Sergeant please do me the honor of signing up Master Andrew Anders into the Union Army as Private

Anders. Good day gentlemen." Nick turned and headed towards the Mercyville Station Telegraph Office.

"Now, if it isn't Master Andrew Anders standing before me." Digger looked the young man up and down as if he was a horse of the dubious kind.

Andy half expected him to open his mouth and guess his age by counting the number of teeth he has, but the sergeant did not do that. Instead, he grinningly proclaimed, "Don't worry lad. You look fit enough to me, just a bit underfed, not to worry. We'll take care of that soon enough. I have some paperwork right here which will change your life and your style of dress forever too."

With a twinkle in his eye and a mischievous grin, he reached into his knapsack and pulled out a handful of rolled up crumpled forms. As he unrolled and paged through his papers, he muttered, "I have a blank enlistment form here somewhere. Ah got it." Uncrumpling and straightening out a piece of paper, he passed it over to Andy, "Here you go. Fill this paper out the best you can and in two minutes you will no longer be a Master of the Universe, but a private at the bottom of the manure pile in the Union Army."

Andy examined the uncrumpled form, "Hmm, I didn't think it would be this easy to sign up. All it wants is my name, hometown, next of kin and a witness. Oh, and dates too … Ah! Sergeant Palgrave, do you have another copy? This one is already filled out." With that said, Andy smiled and handed it back to him.

Palgrave thought for a moment, "Hmm, I don't suppose you want to sign up as yourself, do you? Alright, be different! Most recruits do it incognito, and don't worry about birth date, most recruits get it wrong." He sighed and dug back through his papers, and then quickly came up with another paper, "Here's a blank form and my pencil." Andy took it and this time sat down on one of the station benches to fill it out. "Here you go sir, all done. Ah, who's going to witness it?"

Sergeant Palgrave examined it thoroughly, "Yep it looks all in order. Hmm, who is Angela Fishkill Katz on the next of kin line? Is that your mother's maiden name?"

"No, my ma and pa died when I was young, as did the rest of my immediate family. Angela is my girlfriend. My Aunt Abby, who is not my aunt but was a close friend of my mom, raised me. I don't want to burden her in the event of my death. I think I've burdened her enough in this lifetime."

The sergeant looked over the top of the paper at Andy, "Nonsense! There is still plenty of room after Angela's name, so you put your aunt's name right there next to Angela's. She raised you, and I know she still cares about you, right? Fill in her name. And I'll witness it for you." Andy scribbled Abby Bennington Cardstacker.

Grinning broadly, Digger stuck out his hand for Andy to shake. As they shook hands, the young man felt the sergeant's giant hand engulf his much smaller right hand. Andy was momentarily afraid it would be crushed.

Instead, Palgrave lowered his voice and softly said, "Andy you've got a strong grip. Welcome to the Union Army lad, but I must warn you. We do not have much time, and there will be some long days and nights building this camp. You will be learning and doing many different things as the private at the bottom of the heap. It will be considered a dirty job by all, except by the captain and possibly me. The things you learn here will all be things you need to know to survive this Rebellion and the Union Army."

He handed Private Anders a paper stub, "Andy here's your ticket. Do you see that large tent newly erected over there? You take it to Birdy, our most efficient Quartermaster, and he will outfit you with a uniform, equipment, and supplies. Oh, he will also assign you a tent. You just tell him, I said the tent next to mine by the captain's tent. We'll be working late into the night and I am not going to go traipsing through the camp looking for your tent, you got it?" Andy nodded affirmatively. Sergeant Palgrave just stood there quietly studying him and clearing his throat, as if expecting Andy to say something to him. "Andy, I don't have all night! Aren't you forgetting to do something?"

Looking very perplexed at the sergeant, "I don't think so sir."

"Ah Hah! Finally, the magic word. Good. Dismissed private, and don't forget that again." The sergeant turned from his new private and headed over to the Mercyville Telegraph Office looking for Nick, his Captain."

Andy stood there for a moment trying to figure out what just happened. Finally, it dawned on him that he forgot to say, "Yes sir." He shook his head chuckling as he headed in the direction of the Quartermaster tent.

BEEHIVE OF ACTIVITY

Everywhere Andy looked he noticed something different was going on around him. The men acted like a swarm of busy bees: moving, building or assembling everything all at once everywhere in camp.

In the distance, he heard three whistles cry out from a steam engine signaling the arrival of another troop or supply train. Everyone dropped what they were doing and ran to the train. Andy figured it must have been the much-needed camp supplies arriving on the train. Later on, he would find out that he was right.

He stopped in front of a tent with a wooden plank hung above the entrance, "Quartermaster."

He smiled, for this must be the place. It had every possible type of barrel, wooden crate, dry goods and equipment piled high around it, and all were numbered or marked. He tried reading some of the markings, but they made no sense to him. He thought to himself: I am not here to take inventory, but to get outfitted.

Andy strode into the Quartermaster tent only to discover that it was no haven from bedlam. Instead, the inside looked and felt like chaos with everyone shouting at once over everyone else. He saw a line of young men already signing up, just as he did a few steps away from here. He figured it would be safer in numbers than trying to get something on his own, so he got in line with them.

Andy spotted a tall, lanky uniformed officer walking up and down the side of the line talking to each recruit and checking their tickets. With all these young men signing up this morning, Andy was surprised at how fast Woody's abolitionist newspaper got the word out to Mercyville about the volunteer army.

He was even more surprised at the turn out of the number of young men who wanted to volunteer to put down the Rebellion. Andy felt in his heart that he was doing the right thing. He also knew he had to be in the right tent because all their tickets looked similar to Andy's scrap of paper that Digger had given him.

As Andy stood in line, he felt a sharp pointed uncomfortable poking on his shoulder blade. He turned around, and his grin turned into a frown when he saw it was Francis Franklin Falsemouth, "Morning Andrew. I see they are scraping the bottom of the barrel signing you up."

The two young men next to Francis snickered along with him. Startled to see the three of them there Andy asked, "Francis, how did you and your younger cohorts hear about this signup so fast?"

Francis snidely remarked, "Andrew, we are not blind to the times. We got eyes, and we read the newspaper headlines posted on the Mercyville Republican front door, too. Didn't you hear, I am a natural born leader, and these two fine specimens are volunteering to be in my elite killer squad, unlike you? You have no one, not even a father."

Andy turned around in disgust trying to ignore Francis's snobbishness. Andy stepped forward in line.

From directly behind him, he heard, "Andrew, move a bit faster. You're holding up the war."

His stomach turned when he heard their mocking laughs. Andy thought it was best to ignore the bullies and mind his own business in the long line as it kept moving.

The tall, lanky officer overheard the sarcasm aimed at Andy by the other three young men, when he got to Andy, he politely asked, "Ticket please?"

He reached out for Andy's ticket. He did not say anything else to Andy, or the three smirking young men behind Andy. The tent space full of recruits was droning with activity. It was as if all their voices merged into the sound of bees buzzing around their hive entrance. All of them were trying to get inside at the same time.

The officer stood there for a moment examining Andy's ticket, and he started walking away from Andy without saying another word. Andy raced after the officer as he ducked under a tent flap. It was quieter in there, "According to this ticket stub you are Private Andrew Adam Anders, assigned to Sergeant Palgrave. The sergeant insists that the Quartermaster is to outfit you ASAP."

The officer showed Andrew the ASAP on his scrap of paper and pleasantly smiled, "I'm Quartermaster Bartholomew Binghamton Birdkowski. My friends call me Birdy for short. What do they call you?"

Andy had to think about a nickname. He never had a nickname, and he did not know what to tell Birdy. He did not want to appear snobbish or foolish, nor get off on the wrong foot with Birdy.

After pondering the idea of a nickname, Andy decided to be truthful, "Birdy, I think calling me Andy would do just fine. Nobody ever called me by a nickname before. What do you think?"

Birdy saw Andy was sincere in his innocence, "I'll tell you what. As I fill this order for you, you think about it. Make sure it is a good nickname, not something crappy, but a good name you would like to be called by your friends or a name you would call someone you respect, Okay? By the way who were those three young men behind you?"

Andy sighed and responded to him, "Francis Falsemouth and his two twin buddies, Alfie and Ethan. Why do you ask?"

Birdy calmly replied, "In the captain's unit we all need to work together to get the job done." Then quickly changing the subject he added, "Oh, by the way, why don't you stay here while I get your supplies. Some of those recruits would slit your throat to get an outfit even five minutes before I get to them."

Andy grinned and said, "It sounds like a plan to me. Thank you, Birdy. Oh, how did you get your nickname?"

Birdy laughed loudly, "You crack me up, Andy! With my last name Birdkowski, I'm just glad they didn't think of calling me Cow." With that said, Birdy continued laughing as he disappeared under another tent flap.

Andy smiled widely, at the thought of someone being called Cow. While Andy waited, his stomach grumbled. Except for this morning's cookie, in all the excitement he'd forgotten to eat.

"Andy, while I get the rest of your supplies and equipment, try on this uniform. I take a bit of pride in guessing clothing sizes, and this blue wool uniform looks about the right size and should fit you. It's supplied by the State of Connecticut and is supposed to have already been prewashed. It had better not shrink too much when you wash it the first time. That is why it's a little bit baggy. Go on try it on and I'll be right back with the rest of your equipment."

Before Andy could thank Birdy, he already had slipped out under another tent flap and disappeared. Andy tossed his street clothes into a pile and donned the new uniform. Birdy was right, as he predicted the pants and jacket fitted a little bit baggy. With cap and boots, Andy would be fully dressed.

Feeling tired, he sat down on what looked like a beer keg. Before he knew it, Birdy came back carrying an armful of supplies with a pair of boots on top of the pile. He put the stuff on top of a crate, "Alright, here's a bedroll, knapsack, and backpack. I packed it for you. So, pay extra special attention to how it is packed, or you'll end up with your mess tin and water canteen in the bottom when you need them the most."

He looked at Andy's high arches, "These boots have no arches in them and are designed for one shape to fit both feet. I'm trying to order boots that fit just left or right feet. Until I get them in stock, I am giving everyone an extra pair of socks. When you put on your socks, roll the extra pair up and stuff it in your sock and then wedge it under your arch before you put your boots on. It takes a bit of doing, but it is worth it as you do not want blisters on long marches, right?"

Andy sat there rolling up one sock and stuffing it into the other as Birdy said to do. He struggled to get each boot on, but he did it, "Birdy, your right. It feels weird, but I think it will work. Thank you."

Birdy showed Andy how to pack everything up. Andy put it on and could just about stand with everything crammed into his new backpack or hanging from it. "I think this thing weighs more than I do Birdy. Oh, I thought about a nickname and for now please just call me Andy."

Birdy checked off the ticket, "Alright, I'll log that in my memory." Birdy stopped talking and closed his eyes. He mumbled something and opened them again, "I just remembered, you get to share a tent in the officer's area near Nick and Digger. Okay?"

Then Birdy added, "You will be bunking with Hightop. Just be careful he chews that Maine spruce gum and he sticks it under everything to save for later. Of course, he forgets where he stuck it. One time he helped me move some molasses kegs, and a day or two later, I discovered a wad of that stuff cemented two kegs of molasses together. I had to get a crowbar and pry them apart!"

Andy laughed and had forgotten who Digger was, "Birdy, excuse me for asking, but who's Digger?"

"Oh! Sergeant Palgrave didn't tell you his nickname, did he?"

Andy surmised, "Hmm, that makes perfect sense. After all his last name is pall and grave put together, so Digger would be a natural nickname."

"No, that's not why we call him Digger. It is because when you are under fire you have to dig in fast or die, and he is the fastest foxhole digger you ever did see. His dirt just seems to fly out of the hole just like a dust storm kicks up the earth."

"Oh, that makes sense. Are we done? Birdy, is there anything to sign?" Birdy shook his head no and kept the ticket stub. He gave Andy an envelope addressed to Digger.

Birdy helped Andy out under the tent flap. As Andy headed back towards the captain's tent near the Mercyville Train Station, Birdy headed for Francis Falsemouth. He stepped up to Falsemouth and his buddies, "Gentlemen, may I see your tickets."

All three handed their ticket stubs over to him.

Lying Birdy claimed, "Hmm, I see none of you signed your ticket. You do realize you have not enlisted until you make your mark on it. Here, we can easily rectify that," Birdy quickly handed Falsemouth's ticket stub back to him, "Just initial it, and you're a private at the bottom of the manure pile."

Without thinking Falsemouth initialed his ticket. Birdy quickly snatched it back, "Congratulations Private Falsemouth on signing up to fight the Rebellion, we need more privates like you and your friends to use as cannon fodder for the front lines, and to dig all the latrine pits."

BEEHIVE OF ACTIVITY

On hearing this Francis's two friends, who never did an honest day's work turned green and mumbled in unison to Birdy, "Sorry, we changed our minds, just tear up our tickets."

Alfie and Ethan proceeded to do a quick about-face and ran out of the Quartermaster's tent, leaving Falsemouth to his deviousness, while shouting back at him, "Good riddance Falsemouth! You'll make good cannon fodder!"

Birdy, glad he'd gotten rid of the two young malcontents, smiled as he pocketed their two-worthless ticket stubs.

Next, he turned his attention to his prize catch, Private Falsemouth. Birdy put his hand heavily on the young man's shoulder and guided him out of the line, "Now! Where shall we start? I know we will get you outfitted and I have a lot of dirty oil lamps needing cleaning."

Andy had a hard time walking and lugging everything Birdy had loaded Andy down with on his back. Alfie and Ethan ran past him, neither stopped running until they got back to the tavern across from Woody's newspaper office.

Andy quickly located the officer tents and ducked into the smallest tent. Falling over backward, he dropped his heavy backpack and supplies in the middle of the tent floor. He sat down on one of the cots and started dozing off. After all, Nick and Digger were nowhere around, at least not here anyway.

~ ~ ~

Earlier Nick had turned away from Digger, Nick knew he should have asked the sergeant to find Twitch, but it was too late for that. So, Nick headed down the platform to the station-house and telegraph office.

Luck came Nick's way. Looking between the other soldiers on the platform, he spotted Corporal Harrington Hightop comfortably leaning on the side of the red clapboard station-house, and Nick asked, "Corporal, have you seen Twitch?"

Startled, Hightop slowly looked around for where the voice was coming from. Through the crowd, he spotted the captain heading his way. He spat out his chewed wad of Maine spruce gum and came to attention.

The captain came over to Corporal Hightop, "It's good seeing you Hightop. I don't have much time to explain. Do you know where Twitch is?"

The Corporal thought good and hard for a minute. When he stopped thinking he very slowly replied, "I think he was heading over to the Quartermaster's tent. Or was it for the quarter horses? Maybe it was to mark the quarter mileposts? It was one of them I think."

"Good, I see you're on top of this for me. Corporal! Seek him out, and you shall find him. Now look for him and bring him to me by the telegraph office. He will understand." The corporal stood there ruminating about where to find Twitch when Nick implored, "Corporal! Go Now! Find Twitch for me! Now go! Got it?"

Hightop agreeably nodded his head even though he forgot where Twitch had gotten off to. Finally, he almost remembered, "Yes sir, I'll go get him." Hightop started to leave when he stopped in mid-step, turned and saluted Nick and then sped off.

The captain started to turn away when the sole of his right boot stuck to something on the station platform. He pulled free of the sticky stuff and was scraping it off on the edge of the platform, all the while muttering to himself, "Someday this sticky stuff will cover the world, and all of us will be stuck in one place forever. Even the trains will probably stick to the tracks."

Hightop continued running northward through the crowd of soldiers on his search mission to find Twitch.

He ran straight to the Quartermaster tent ducking under the tent flap and shouting, "Birdy, is Twitch out back?"

Birdy had his hands full lugging two-quarter kegs of whale oil from out back for the oil lamps. Birdy handed off the quarter kegs to Private Falsemouth, who staggered under their weight. "Here you go Private Falsemouth fill all the oil lanterns and lamps, there's about two hundred lanterns needing filling. It will keep you busy most of today."

Birdy turned to Corporal Hightop, "Sorry, you just missed Twitch. He's heading for the Quarter Horses."

With a quick thank you, Hightop was out of the tent faster than a cat can catch a mouse. He kept running all the way to the far side of the camp where the officers' quarter horses are stabled. He spotted Twitch staking out a new line of poles for the base perimeter.

Hightop somewhat out of breath said, "Lieutenant Twitch, Nick needs you at the station telegraph office … He sent me to bring you at once. Come On! Let's Go, Sir!"

Twitch stopped what he was doing and remembered the last time Nick needed him at another telegraph office. Perhaps, Nick was in deep trouble again. "Corporal, let's get going. I think we are going to have our hands full this time. Get on the wagon. We can't have you all out of breath when we get there."

They arrived to see Nick nonchalantly pretending to read his newspaper while waiting patiently near the station office. Twitch got his Colt firearm and holster out of the wagon toolbox. Strapping it on, he felt better about being armed here. He noticed Nick spotted him and then Nick folded up the newspaper.

Twitch whispered, "Thank you Hightop, stay close to me until we find out if Nick needs you too?" Hightop nodded and surreptitiously pointed his thumb down past the captain. Twitch eyed the two men. He silently signaled Nick. Hightop spotted the signal and knew to head around to the back of the station quietly.

Twitch glanced down past the captain at the two men wearing unseasonable long raincoats with unnatural bulges under their armpits. He stepped up to Nick and whispered, "Why Nick, the last time I saw you, weren't you standing by a train station office just like this one here? Also, weren't there two vultures bothering you then too? I see two different vultures have shown up here with the same murderous intent."

Nick whispered, "Sorry Twitch, I didn't expect the mayor to get them here so fast."

"Don't worry sir. I already took precautions. Just make out like we are still talking. We both know they are cowards. I doubt very much if they will try anything until I step away and they have a clear shot."

As they talked, a group of Union soldiers seemed to stroll from around the back of the station. They innocently began pushing and shoving each other. This action caught the eyes of the two men.

Before they knew it, the soldiers were between the captain and the two men. Nick and Twitch heard two bodies gasp as they collapsed, hitting the platform deck. Suddenly the soldiers stepped aside to reveal to their captain both men knocked unconscious by Hightop. He was proudly standing with one foot on the back of one of the would-be assassins, the same as a big game moose hunter in the backwoods of Maine would do.

Nick praised them, "Gentlemen, thank you for your aid in my time of need. Now please gently disarm and detain our prisoners until we have questioned them."

Turning to Twitch, Nick said, "I still need you inside as we're taking over the Mercyville station and telegraph office. I need your team of telegraphers and wire runners to check things out and run things here."

Twitch grinned with approval. "Nick, would you mind if I had my boys pay the telegraph office a small visit first? I get the feeling someone may have left a window or two open, and a vulture or two might be a bit inside."

"Sounds reasonable Lieutenant Twitch. Please carry on." Replied Nick.

Twitch quietly hand signaled his men. A couple of soldiers stepped inside while talking loudly about telegraphing their families. Soon a short, loud scuffle ensued, ending with a body hitting the inside of the station office paned glass window. A moment later, some soldiers dragged two more bodies from the telegraph office and deposited them on top of the first two would-be assassins.

Twitch stepped over to talk to a soldier inside the station office. Once or twice, he nodded his head. It was not long before he hand-signaled the captain to approach, "All clear sir. I understand the station master and telegrapher are rather talkative, at least for the time being.

No telling how much longer they will remain cooperative if you get my drift, sir."

"Lieutenant Twitch have any of your men had the chance to examine the telegraph equipment?"

Twitch thought for a moment before stepping inside the Telegraph Office. A few minutes later he came out from around the back of the building, "Old and outdated sir. However, some odd new wires are running towards the old town hall. Do you want us to check them out?"

Nick ordered, "Before the telegrapher and his assistant change their minds take their statements for me. You'll know if their lying or not, better than I ever would."

Nick paused to think for a moment, "Have your men hold off following the wires for a few minutes. I want to talk to our new Private Andy Anders. He may be able to shed some light on this new information. We have here. By the way, has anyone seen him around?"

Hightop looked up from guarding the pile of unconscious prisoners and shook his head no. Nick ordered, "Hightop, have someone else guard them. I have something more important for you to do. Get over to my tent, see if there is a Private Anders there, and bring him back. Oh, he just might be waiting for us in your tent."

"Yes, sir will do!" Hightop ran off to the officer's tents nearby.

Nick turning to Twitch said, "Twitch, I think it will be too dangerous to go alone. After I talk to Andy, take him and a well-armed contingency force with you. Take about half a dozen crack shots or so and assume whomever you find is armed and dangerous. We're shorthanded, and we need every soldier we have alive, so no heroics by anyone. Understand?"

"Yes, sir." Twitch pointed out a bit surprised, "Hmm, I see Hightop. He's already on his way back with someone, and I do not recognize him."

After trying to keep up with the corporal, Andy arrived a bit winded, "You wanted to talk to me, sir?"

Nick calmly responded, "Yes I do. Private Anders, it is time to find out the depth of your knowledge about the mayor's organization." The captain pointed at the four bodies on the platform, "Do you recognize any of those four unconscious prisoners on the platform?"

Andy walked over to them and squatted down to take a closer look at their faces, "Yes sir, this one is Zebulun Matthews. He is a slave master. These other two are his slave hunters who do his dirty work for him. I made an entry in the mayor's books for Matthews. Come to think of it! He's the one who got a payment the day after my friends disappeared."

Looking at another prisoner, Andy remarked with a bit of surprise in his voice, "Oh my! I think this last one is

Jacob Weedon, a local farmer's son. What is he doing mixed up with this bunch?"

Very pleased with the report, Nick nodded his head in approval. Nick looked up the platform, his attention was now turned on the old town hall. "Andy, why are there telegraph lines running toward the old town hall?"

Andy thought for a moment, then replied, "Last month the mayor cleared us all out of it and had me hire four linesmen and order enough telegraph equipment and batteries to equip four telegraphers, along with the wires, poles, and insulators. I know the main floor is full of shipping crates destined for the new city hall. However, both floors upstairs were emptied out, except for four tables with four old roller chairs." Twitch listened intently to his narration.

The captain asked, "Andy, did you see any guards?" Twitch became doubly interested.

"That's the odd part. During the day there's only one guard inside, an old man named Ham. He sleeps mostly. I have stopped over there on occasion, and he has yet to be awake and he never even knew I was there.

"However, at night there are two guards. One guard sits on the front porch in a rocking chair pretending to whittle. The other guard sits in the kitchen drinking and making coffee for the second-floor telegraphers. They're on duty from six to sunup. At sunup, Ham shows up, and they go home. When he is late, the place is left empty until Ham arrives." Andy's statement perked everyone's ears up.

Twitch asked him, "Are you telling me if we go over to the old town hall right now, there will be just one old man sleeping there?"

Andy nodded in the affirmative. He took out his father's gold pocket watch, "We have about an hour because he sets his alarm for five o'clock, so the telegraphers don't catch him napping."

Andy snapped his gold watch shut and pocketed it. Nick and Twitch caught a glimpse of the gold watch. Andy continued to say, "Ham trusts me and I could take you over there and get his shotgun before he wakes up. If the back door is locked, I still have the spare key and can let you in." He took his keychain out of his pocket and dangled it in Twitches face.

Twitch shook his head in disbelief, "Andy, we're thinking of taking some men over there. Is there anything else we should know?"

Andy smiled, "Sure, the mayor still lives across the street until he finishes his new mansion in town. I think he should be home any minute. So, if you are planning on a raid, we can cut across the tobacco fields to the back gate, and I can let you in the back door. He can't see us approaching the building through the back garden. When the guards and telegraphers arrive later, you can catch them red handed with whatever they're up to."

The captain asked, "Do you think something fishy is going on?"

Andy thought and then rattled off, "Hmm, the other day, Mister Fredericks and Mister Smithers, both members of the town council came into the new town hall and were demanding that the mayor explain the expenses for the new telegraphers. Indignantly the mayor brushed them off. The mayor accused them of being ignorant and not knowing about the transatlantic cable laid in 1858. He showed all of us an old Mercyville Post newspaper clipping from August of 1858 when President Buchanan and Queen Victoria exchanged formal complimentary messages to inaugurate the service. Furthermore, the mayor claimed the telegraphers were contacting and negotiating with the British and European tobacco importers so he could get the best prices for his wrappers."

Twitch angrily chimed in, "Wait a minute! I remember when that cable was laid. It failed about a month later! Nick, I would have heard if it was working again. There is no working transatlantic cable, today!"

Andy nodded in agreement, "I'm telling you, Captain, that is what I found out the other day when I talked to the station telegrapher. He did not know about the cable working either. I am telling you captain just like in Shakespeare's Hamlet where there was something rotten in Denmark, well, this time there's something rotten in Mercyville."

Chapter Four

Andy caught his breath and continued his tale, "Besides, the telegraph office closes after the last train pulls out and doesn't reopen until sunrise. So, I ask myself what kind of messages are four telegraphers sending from the old town hall all night?"

Nick thought out loud, "Andy maybe it's not what they are transmitting, but rather whose messages are they trying to intercept and listen in on?"

A NARROW ESCAPE

Nick Cautioned Twitch, "Alright, take half a dozen sharpshooters and follow Andy through the back way over to the kitchen door of the old town hall. Andy, I need you to go in and disarm Ham any way you can. Use your head and err on the side of safety."

He continued, "Andy, Twitch will be there to back you up. If you get cornered, just take your cap off, and Twitch will have a sharpshooter take Ham out."

Andy started to object because Ham was his friend, but he thought better of it. "Yes, sir."

"Come on Andy." Twitch paused for a moment while thinking and then enquired, "Andy, we have what, about fifteen minutes to get over there and get this done, so no one gets hurt?"

CHAPTER FIVE

Andy agreed and without another word said, he led the six of them off the platform and toward the tobacco fields. "Be careful of your footing. The soil is freshly turned over, and it is easy to sprain or break your ankle out here in one of these uneven furrows."

They made it to the back gate of the rose garden behind the old town hall kitchen. Twitch placed his sharpshooters along the old wooden garden fence.

Twitch spied that the back door was wide-open and nudged Andy, "This might be easier than we think. Look."

Andy took a good look and noticed Ham still sound asleep with his feet up on the table, but Andy could not see Hams' shotgun. He whispered to Twitch, "We're in luck! He's still out cold. Quick, follow me in!"

Andy made for the open door and raced up the steps in a flash with Twitch right behind him. Once inside, Andy spotted Ham's old shotgun leaning in a corner. Andy made for it just as Ham's alarm sounded.

Ham woke up to Twitch standing over him. Twitch pointed a Colt forty-five directly between Ham's eyes. Ham angrily said, "What in tarnation are you doing? Didn't your Momma teach you not to point a gun at people cause it might go off by accident?"

Sighing Twitch said, "Old man, I only point it when I don't trust who I am pointing it at and right now it is you. So, behave yourself, and I will give you a silver dollar in the morning. Now be good and follow Andy out the back door and do as he says, and you'll get another dollar."

A bit frustrated, "My name is Ham, and not the old man." He spotted Andy in the corner with his shotgun, "Oh! Hi Andy. I didn't see you over there. Ah, how come you got my shotgun?"

Twitch smiled, "No time for pleasantries. You two can talk about it on the way back to the station. Now get out of here! Come on! Out! Out! Out, both of you, I got serious work to do."

As Andy and Ham headed for the garden back gate, two of the sharpshooters passed them heading towards the kitchen.

Ham asked Andy, "Is he truly going to give me a silver dollar?"

"Yes, Ham. Now we have to be quiet and get out of here. Watch your step cutting across the field. I don't want you hurt." As they headed across the field, six more soldiers with muskets in hand passed by as they followed Andy and Twitch's footprints toward the old town hall.

Andy stopped with Ham, and Andy hollered to the private in the lead, "What's your big hurry?"

They heard back only a one-word reply from one of the passing soldiers, "Reinforcements!"

On the way back, Ham needed to stop and rest a couple of times. It took Andy a lot longer to hike back with Ham than when he led Twitch to the old town hall.

Ham started to huff and puff all out of breath as he crossed over the rows of tilled soil while trying to keep up with Andy. Concerned, Andy asked. "Ham, are you going to be alright? You ain't got consumption, do you?"

"Oh no Andy, I ain't got consumption. I'm not so fast anymore because age catches up with you, and robs you of your youth."

"Ok, let's stop for another break, and just you remember I got your shotgun."

Ham reached into his pants pocket, "Andy, you're a good kid. I wouldn't do anything to hurt you, especially shoot you with a loaded shotgun."

Ham showed Andy the two shotgun shells in his hand, "Andy I never keep that old thing loaded because I might knock it over in my sleep. The last thing I want is for people to think someone killed me with it. Worse yet, thinking I killed myself when it might have been a dumb accident. Ah, why don't you want the shells?"

Andy shook his head in disbelief, "Nah, they're safer in your pocket. Besides I'd probably trip in one of these ruts and blow my foot off, or worse yet the back of your head."

Ham laughed, "Good point I sure don't want a bald spot back there. I think I'll just keep them shells awhile longer. You're learning kid. You're going to be a survivor in this here coming war with the rebels, whenever that happens."

"Ham what do you think of the Rebellion?"

Ham stopped walking again, but this time to think out loud, "Since October, last year, a lot of my friends lost their jobs. I cannot get a steady job except for hustling up part-time work now and again. I do not think there are enough jobs for people, so I wonder what do we need slaves for these days? I just do not understand slavery. It doesn't help anybody."

They finally arrived back to the train station, and it was pretty much deserted except for the four bushwhackers and their guards. Andy saw the captain step out of the telegraph office reading a dispatch, and Oldstone said, "Look what the cat dragged in. Good job Andy. You must be Ham. Welcome to the Union Army, sir."

Ham grinned, "A pleasure to meet you too, sir." He added questioningly, "I take it you've seized the tobacco plantation, and are now making it your home?"

While still looking at the dispatch, Nick commented, "You're very observant Ham. Tell me, what were you guarding that is so important to the mayor?"

Chapter Five

Ham confidently replied, "Why all the crates on the first floor of the old town hall of course."

Nick asked, "I see, and did you open any of them?"

Ham just stood there quietly, not answering him.

While the captain patiently awaited Ham's answer, he stepped over to the telegraph office doorway, "Digger, please step out here for a moment."

The captain turned back toward them, "Andy, that's a nice old shotgun. Our men need a break, so use it to guard the prisoners."

Digger ducked under the top of the doorframe and stepped onto the platform. Andy handed Digger the envelop from Birdy and then walked down to the four prisoners.

Nick quietly asked Digger, "I would appreciate it if you would help Ham to remember what he saw in the crate he opened."

"Me sir? Twitch will be …"

Nick interrupted him, "Yes Digger. Remember, you taught me not to repeat myself. Now see to his immediate needs. I am sure you can negotiate quickly with him for any additional information he may have.

"Excuse me, gentlemen, I need to reply to an urgent telegram." With that said, Nick stepped into the telegraph office.

Digger stood there for a moment or two thinking, "Ham, would you care for some coffee?"

Ham shook his head no, "But I'll have the silver dollar the tall, thin soldier offered me if I behaved."

Andy chimed in, "Digger, Twitch told Ham he would get a silver dollar in the morning if he went along with me and behaved."

"Oh, I see." Digger slid his hand into his pocket and stepped over to Ham, handing him two silver dollars.

Ham looked at them strangely, "No he said one, not two." Ham put one in his pocket and went to give the other one back to Digger.

Digger calmly said, "Ham answer the captain's question, and you get to keep both silver dollars."

At first, Ham was puzzled by the two coins. However, very soon an enlightened look appeared on his face, "Oh I get it! What was in the crate I opened? Here I better give you these thingamajigs."

Ham reached into his pocket and handed Digger a fistful of unstamped brass coin blanks about the size of silver dollars. The sergeant looked them over, "Brass slugs? Any idea why the mayor is trying to hide them, or what he is going to do with these coin blanks?"

"I don't know. I only found these things in the one crate I opened." Ham went all-quiet again.

"Ham, would another silver dollar help jog your memory of what the mayor put in the other crates by chance?"

Ham sighed, "No sir. I didn't look into any others, but I know where they hid those crates. They buried them in …"

A commotion broke out by the prisoners. Matthews, the slave master, knocked Andy to the ground. He pointed Ham's shotgun at Andy's head. "Let all the prisoners go, or I'll kill him," he screamed at all the blue coats surrounding them.

Digger instinctively pushed Ham gently out of the line of fire and slowly moved closer towards Matthews. Suddenly Andy reached up. Pushing the barrel of the shotgun away from his face and grabbing the front of the barrel, he pulled down hard on it towards the station platform. Matthews squeezed both triggers, only to hear the click of the triggers as both barrels misfired.

Matthews lost his balance, falling on top of Andy. He rolled off and was half-way up when Digger reached him. Digger's fist struck Matthews with a short, hard, jab to the jaw. Matthews wobbled from the excruciating pain as his knees buckled and he collapsed out cold once again. Andy got up, "Thanks, Sergeant, but I was in no real danger, Ham's shotgun ain't loaded."

Digger picked up the shotgun and cocked back both triggers into place. Pointing the gun towards the sky, he pulled both triggers. The sound of both barrels going off was deafening to anyone nearby. He opened the breach and ejected both shotgun shells, "Yeah right Andy!"

Digger showed Andy the now empty gun barrels. "You're really lucky it's an old gun. Be grateful …"

Digger snapped the breach closed and did not pull back on both hammers. Next, aiming high in the sky he pulled the triggers and both hammers miss fired."

"As I said be grateful Matthews didn't know with this old shotgun you have to cock both hammers back fully before pulling the triggers. If he did, we would be burying you without a face in the cemetery bright and early tomorrow morning."

Andy reached over and picked up the two still warm shotgun shells. Turning them repeatedly, it suddenly dawned on him, and he cried out "I coulda been killed! Ham! You told me it wasn't loaded!"

Sheepishly Ham grinned as he scratched his jaw thinking, "Oh that's where I put the other two shells. Sorry. Andy, I did not mean to scare you. I only forgot where I put them."

Andy turned as white as a ghost. He sat down on the station's wooden platform clutching the shells in his hands mumbling, "I coulda been killed."

Someone came up behind him. Andy recognized Nick's calm voice, "Andy, Ham's forgetful and he almost got you killed. Take a deep breath and remember never trust anyone when it comes to loaded guns. You must open the weapon and see for yourself that it is not loaded. Now apologize to Ham. You hurt his feelings, and he doesn't know any better."

Andy, without really thinking about it mumbled an apology.

The captain turned towards Ham, "I heard what you said about the crates being buried. Ham, we need those crates. Please lead Sergeant Palgrave to where they're buried." Ham nodded and smiled at the captain.

"Digger, you'll need a couple of very able-bodied soldiers like yourself to recover those crates."

Crouching down behind Andy, Nick quietly asked him, "Andy, are you going to be alright? I need your help. Twitch sent us a telegram from the old town hall. It says he found something important, and for me to go over there right away." Andy just sat on the station platform staring at the two shells in his hand.

Digger came over, "Nick is Andy alright?"

"I'm not sure. Andy keeps staring at the shotgun shells in his hands. I guess he is still in shock."

"Hmm, I don't know what the Doc would call it, but I think he's daydreaming of death. I've seen this before. We've got to wake him up before death is all he can think about." Digger lifted his foot and gave Andy a good sharp shove on the back of his shoulder with the sole of his boot. The force of the blow shook Andy to the bone and Digger loudly, demanded, "Andy! Wake UP!"

The jolt seemed to wake him from his deep thoughts. Andy turned and looked up at the sergeant, "Oh, hi sergeant. Is it morning already?"

Nick pointed off in the distance, "Come on Andy time to go. Take the lead to the old town hall because Twitch needs your help."

Andy got up and started walking towards the old town hall, and Nick followed him.

THE HIDDEN AGENDA

Digger looked about for any soldier looking idle to make up his small work crew, but the only ones on the platform were the guards with their prisoners. "Well, well, well, I think I found me a work crew. Guards bring the prisoners. Something tells me that you are going to unbury what you probably buried in the first place. Come on, follow Ham and me."

Ham led them right through the middle of the camp. On the way, Digger stopped off at the Quartermaster's tent, "Birdy, fetch me a wagon and a dozen or so shovels. If you have any grub axes, throw them in our order too. I also need a dozen or so privates for digging and carting and doing guard duty."

Birdy shouted orders to his privates. They waited a while before Isaac Johnson the lead teamster brought up a wagon for Digger's expedition. "Birdy, here's your wagon, and Jankowski will be driving for you."

Birdy's men loaded shovels, spades and grub axes for the growing expedition. Birdy even threw in a dozen whale oil lanterns for the fading day.

Ham, the prisoners, the guards, the privates, and the mule-drawn wagons made up quite a procession. As they passed right through the middle of camp, someone jokingly shouted out, "Hey Digger! You're going in the wrong direction! The Rebellion's in the South, not the North." Everyone within earshot broke into laughter, even Ham and the guards.

Digger shouted back, "Thanks for volunteering for latrine duty. Grab your shovel and join us." Everyone roared back in even louder laughter.

The expedition reached about halfway between the camp and the line of tobacco barns in the north. "Ham, where are we going? Why do you keep stopping? Did you lose your way?"

"No, sir. I'm just getting my bearings. We go between those two barns right there. See, you can just make out the oldest oak tree on the plantation between those two barns."

Chapter Six

Digger pointed between two of the barns. "Everyone, you heard Ham! Let's move out. Ham, get on the wagon with Jankowski, you've earned a free ride."

Ham rather straightforward asked. "And I get another silver coin, right?"

Digger looked askance at him, "Ham, we are not on a toll road where I pay you every few feet. It will all depend on what we find out there under the old tree."

It was not long before they reached the tree. Digger noticed a long depression on the ground. "Ham, it looks like a lot of something was buried just below the surface over here. Is this the spot?

"No sir, not there." Ham pointed up ahead at a tree. "Over there under the east side of that old oak tree."

Ham got off the wagon and limped over to the tree. He stopped next to a small pile of stones. "I watched that slave master, and those prisoners put some crates right here in the ground. After they left, I snuck back and piled these stones right here, so I would not forget the spot."

Digger started shouting orders out. "Men! Break out the shovels and grub axes. As they say in dueling 'choose your weapons.' Guards, chain their ankles and give them shovels. I do not trust the prisoners with the grub axes — save them for the recruits."

One of the prisoners started arguing with a guard and started a shoving match with him. The prisoner angrily shouted, "I ain't going to do it. I may have buried them, but those three murderers can dig up the bodies of the men they murdered!"

Hearing this everyone froze, because they knew it was bad luck disturbing the dead and buried, murdered or not.

"Hold on! Everyone stay right where you are." Digger made his way over to the prisoner, "What's your name? Come on, answer my question! You accused your mates of murder. Knowing about it makes you either an accomplice or a cooperative witness. You have one chance to clear your name, and you had better take it, or I will personally hang you from this old oak tree myself. Now talk!"

"I'm Jacob Weedon." Pointing to the slave master, "Zebadiah Matthews ordered me to bury the crates from the old town hall. I had just finished digging the hole."

Jacob pointed at the other prisoners, "When these three showed up in a wagon with five strangers whom I never laid eyes on before, they were all hogtied. Zeb, Marcus, and Williams kicked and shoved the five prisoners out of the wagon and lined them up alongside my hole. Zeb proceeded to joke about them being Irish and Italian papists while Marcus and Williams clubbed and horsewhipped those poor men. I watched in horror as Zeb, and the others laughingly took turns shooting each in the back of the head, dead."

Tears streamed down Jacob's cheeks as he finished his story, "They fell into the hole that I dug for the crates. I ain't killed no one. There are no crates in that hole, only those poor dead men."

All the soldiers listening to Jacob's tale were appalled. As soldiers, they want to die in battle but to hear of this atrocity was heart-wrenching.

Digger sincerely asked, "You swear to God in front of all present you witnessed this?"

Jacob nodded his head in the affirmative, still looking down at his shoes and the dusty ground.

Digger gently took Jacob by his chin and lifted up his face until he could look into his tear-filled eyes. "Lad, you have to swear it out loud, or you're one of them."

Jacob quietly replied, "I swear on the Bible sir."

It was dead quiet except for the shovel noises from the three prisoners ignoring the story, as they coldly dug out the pit.

Digger turned to the guards, "Take him over by the barn and protect him. No one is to talk to him or visit him. He is in protective custody. Do not leave his side, no matter what, and do not let him mix with any of the recruits. One might be a rebel spy and try to kill him."

A guard yelled out, "Hey! A prisoner hit something!"

Digger came over to the pit and could make out part of a pant leg. Sarcastically, Matthews mouthed-off unremorsefully, "You want us to dig around it or what?" Digger's fist struck Matthew's jaw hard. The force dropped him with a thud into the pit on top of the pant leg.

Digger angrily roared, "You in the pit! Get Matthews out of there! Drag him over there by the oak tree. No, on second thought, tie Matthews up to the tree good and tight, and pile all those dead men in front of him. I want him to sit there and see his dirty work."

The two prisoners pulled Matthews out and then dragged the limp corpses out of the pit, one by one. Altogether there were five corpses in total. Talking to the guards, Digger coldly whispered, "Make sure all the prisoners are still here when I get back. I want them alive for the captain. I need to get some fresh air. Something around here stinks, and it's not yet the corpses."

Digger lowered his voice and whispered to the guard, "Ham led us to the bodies, thinking they were crates. Keep an eye on him and find out in a friendly way if he knows where the crates are buried."

The guard with the stone face asked, "Digger, who do you think the dead men are?"

Digger did not say anything for about a minute, "I don't know, but I think maybe Andy knows. If you need me, I'm heading over to the old town hall to have a little talk with Andy and the captain about this."

Digger quickly added, "I'll be gone for a while. Watch your back with our prisoners. I think it would be a good idea to keep them digging while I'm gone, understand?"

Stone Face, the guard, did not have to say a word. He had that look of understanding on his face. Digger started walking back over the fields gradually drifting towards the old town hall.

~~~

In the meantime, Andy and the captain arrived at the rose garden back entrance to the old town hall. Nick sensed something was wrong and kept Andy from entering the garden through the gate. Very quietly, just above a whisper, the captain said, "Andy! Wait here a minute."

Nick drew his weapon and stealthily moved through the half-open gate. Very slowly he made his way up to the steps. Inside Nick could hear someone trying to pry open a crate. As he made his way up the weathered back porch steps, a step creaked revealing him. Inside he heard shuffling and a door slamming.

Nick knew he had lost the chance at surprise, as he quickly stepped to the side of the door frame. "Twitch, where are you? Twitch! Where's our guard?"

In answer, Nick heard a man running outside toward the back of the house and suddenly stop just before the corner. "Nick is that you?"

"If it weren't, I'd have shot you through the wall by now. The guard is gone, and there is someone inside trying
~~~

to get into the crates. Twitch, do you want the honors or not?"

Twitch came around the corner fast and took the steps two at a time, kicking the door open and diving inside. No shots or any noise from inside followed Twitch's actions. Nick waited, but Twitch was still silent. "Twitch, are you alright?"

Nick heard a low voice. "Shh! Wait a minute. I'm busy. Okay, it's safe for you to come in for now."

Edging his way in, Nick spotted Twitch examining the guard on the floor. He looked up at Nick, "Marty's been knocked out, but he should be alright. You said you heard someone in here?"

With his revolver still out, Nick whispered, "When I came up the steps, I heard a prying sound and a door slamming inside the building. Twitch, what did you do with the other guards and extra men?"

"Our guards are well concealed, six outside and four on the third floor. All of them are waiting for my signal. The telegraphers have not shown up yet. They're late. They should be here any minute."

Somewhat unsure Nick asked, "Twitch, which door do the telegraphers use to get in?"

Twitch cringed. "Oops! Andy said we need to leave the back door open for them." Thinking quickly, "Come on before it's too late. Help me move Marty into the front room. We'll hide in there behind the crates."

They quickly dragged the unconscious Marty out of the kitchen and hid with him behind some large crates. They just settled in when they heard Andy speaking rather loudly outside. "Hey! What's the idea of being late? Yah right! Ham left a long time ago. The mayor is sure going to love it when I tell him you're all late. Don't give me any lip! You know as well as I do, the mayor will dock your time. Now get in there and get to work."

Nick and Twitch heard the four telegraphers quickly stomping up the back stoop, and noisily banging into the back door as they came inside. They listened to the telegraphers tear down the hallway and start up the creaky stairs. Twitch waited until he heard the sound of footsteps in the room above before taking a deep breath and blowing his old police whistle. Nick cringed from the piercing scream of the whistle.

The front door slammed open against the wall, as a mob of blue-coat soldiers raced up the stairs.

Twitch and Nick grinned as the noisy brawl broke out on the second floor. The fighting over their heads sounded as if all pandemonium had broken out up there. The foot thumping and furniture smashing echoed down the stairs, followed by the sounds of bodies hitting the bare wooden flooring overhead.

Ceiling plaster and dust rained down on top of Twitch and Nick and all over the crates. From all the foot stomping fighting above them, it sounded as if a battle royal was going on.

Together, they both realized that it turned dead silent, except for some real heavy breathing echoing down the stairwell. Still holding the old police whistle, Twitch grinned, "Nick, I think we got them." Twitch started getting up out of his hiding place when he was knocked over by a figure running past them and out the kitchen door.

They heard a scream and a crashing noise out back, "Oh! No!" Nick yelled. "I forgot about Andy!"

They charged out the back door to discover Andy standing triumphantly beside an upside-down wheelbarrow on top of an unconscious figure. Twitch exclaimed, "Andy! What in tarnation happened out here?"

Andy stood there with a hoe poking the back of the man's head sticking out from under the wheelbarrow. Hearing the kitchen door slam shut, Andy turned around toward Nick and Twitch. All Andy could do was scream frightfully from the sight of them. He quickly came to his senses when he realized the two of them were only covered in white dust.

Catching his breath, Andy exclaimed, "Wow! You two gave me such a start! I thought you were both ghosts coming after me!"

Nick and Twitch took a good look at each other and realized they were covered head to toe in white ceiling dust. At this point, they could not keep a straight face. Soon they began to laugh hysterically. Both turned toward Andy, "Ooool We've come for you, Private Andy!"

They grabbed their sides from laughing too hard and had to wipe the tears from their eyes. They smeared the tear streaks down their cheeks, making them appear more like ghoulish clowns rather than Union officers.

Taking a deep breath, the captain composed himself first. "Sorry Andy, we couldn't help it. Now you were saying?"

"I didn't do nothing much. I just pushed the garden wheelbarrow in front of Mayor Katz as he raced out the back door. He did the rest by falling head over heels on it. Somehow the wheelbarrow ended up on top of him with a little bit of help from me, of course."

With hoe in hand, Andy mischievously grinned as he poked the mayor again. Nick, Andy, and Twitch started laughing at the mayor because with the wheelbarrow on top of him. He looked like a giant unconscious Galapagos tortoise lying face down.

One of the soldiers came down from upstairs and spotted them in the backyard. He went out and headed over to Twitch, "Sir, we got five all tied up: four telegraphers and one guard. That's all there is sir. To be safe, we checked every room in there, even the cold cellar.

We even bayoneted the coal in the coal bin. Do you want us to bring the prisoners down and out back here?"

Twitch looked at Nick, who silently shook his head no. Twitch thought for a minute, "You caught just one guard not two?" The soldier nodded yes, "Okay, we'll be up in a minute."

In a lowered voice, Twitch asked Andy, "Don't look around. Have you seen anyone else out here?"

Just audibly, Andy whispered hesitantly, "No. Ah, maybe we should all take cover inside."

Whispering just as softly, Nick asked, "Twitch, do we have any sharpshooters still out here?"

Twitch stretched and slowly took off his hat to wipe his brow. To those who knew him, it was an unmistakable signal to their guards keeping a lookout for the mayor's hired sharpshooters."

"Nick, one of those rebels might be waiting out there with a long rifle and a chance to shoot you. Let's not give him that opportunity for murder. Step easily between Andy and me, and then all of us will quietly move into the house through the back door together. Okay?"

Andy asked Nick, "What about Katz?"

"Leave him there. It looks like he's out for the count until morning. Anyway, I'll feel better once we're inside."

They headed for the steps, with Nick stepping between them. Twitch stepped behind the captain, and the captain bent down low, as he rushed up the stairs and into the kitchen.

Once all were inside the kitchen, Andy closed and locked the back door. Twitch raced straight through the kitchen to the hallway and up the stairs. Nick quietly slipped into the front room where the window shades were down all day.

Andy felt like he had missed something about the mayor and Nick, "Captain, what's going on? You're not telling me something."

"Andy, let's just say I spoiled our friend the mayor's plans for Mercyville, and he wants to get me out of the way. All I can do is to wait for Twitch's sharpshooter to do his …" He stopped in mid-sentence when a shot echoed down from upstairs.

Nick raced to the bottom of the stairs and hollered, "Twitch, are you guys okay up there?" His voice echoed throughout the house.

Nick backed away from the stairs when two soldiers charged down the stairs followed by Twitch. The two soldiers headed out the front door.

Twitch stopped and excitedly proclaimed, "I think we got him, sir. Someone was in the tree across the street. My man on the roof saw a dark shape in it, so he took the shot with his Sharps rifle. He told me, he saw a musket fall out of the tree, and a moment later a body. We're going over to find out who he was and to secure the area. You'd better wait here until I give the all clear."

Nick nodded his head in agreement. Andy just sat on a crate in disbelief, thinking people hide in trees to kill other people.

The two of them sat waiting in silence for Twitch to return. They heard footsteps coming up the front porch steps and towards the front door. "It's all clear sir. He's the only one."

Twitch opened the front door, "You can both come out now. Andy, take a look at him and see if you can identify him or not?"

As they both followed Twitch across the street, Andy asked, "Twitch, where did your man shoot him from?"

"There's a small trap door on the back roof. Max, my shooter, climbed up to the roof peak. There was just enough half moonlight to spot a weak reflection off of any shiny surface down below. Max did not see any reflection. He was about to give the all clear when he noticed a branch shiver with no wind. He waited until the branch shivered again, and aimed at the crook of the tree branch and fired. You know the rest, Andy."

When they reached the body, one of Twitch's men held a whale oil lantern to illuminate the upturned face of the dead man. "Andy, do you know him?"

Andy stared at the corpse's cold dead eyes. He spotted the deep red scar cutting across the chin up to the left eyebrow. "Yea. I have seen him around, but he is not the other guard. I don't know his name. Last month I accidentally interrupted him and Katz arguing. Katz stopped him from throwing me out of the office window. It was the one-time Katz helped me, and I just wish I overheard what they were arguing about."

Twitch stood there quietly for a while before he went through the dead man's pockets, but the only thing in the pockets was lint. "That's odd, I'd expected to find at least a penknife, pocket watch or maybe some pocket change, but nothing Nick, nothing at all."

A sharp short whistle broke the silence. Twitch spun around and raced back to the old town hall. He headed around back.

Andy and Nick caught up with Twitch in the backyard talking to another soldier.

They immediately noticed someone had turned the wheelbarrow upright and the mayor was gone. The soldier left, and Twitch turned to them. "We solved the mystery of the missing guard. He was hiding in the tool shed. After we left, he ran out and rescued the mayor. He had to skirt the outside of our perimeter not to get shot by any of us or his sniper in the tree."

Andy asked Twitch, "Why didn't our man stop him?"

Twitch apologized, "My man was too far out back trying to keep a low profile in the field, in case anyone was trying to sneak up on us. The guard picked the perfect moment to grab the mayor. He waited until a small cloud passed over the half-moon. My man didn't have any moonlight to shoot under, he had just enough to see the shadowy movement."

Nick sighed, "Don't worry Andy, we'll get him another time. It's getting late, and besides, we have some prisoners to question upstairs."

Coming through the back-gate, Digger interrupted Nick, "Captain you may want to leave that until morning. We did not find the crates, but we did find five buried corpses. According to Jacob Weedon, it looks like Matthews did them in and hid the bodies. I can fill you in on the way back."

Nick sighed, "Andy, with what you told me about your missing friends, I had a suspicion that when Ham said he saw them burying crates, I feared it might be something other than crates. I was hoping I was wrong."

He added, "We might as well head over there and find out who they dug up. Andy, if they are who I think they are, I will need you to identify them positively.

"Digger, let's go. As we walk back, you can fill me in as to how you found the bodies."

Nick stopped in mid-stride, "Hold on a minute." He shouted out, "Hey Twitch! Where's my horse? He should have been unloaded by now from the boxcar. Have one of your men bring over a couple of horses for us."

Jokingly to the captain, Twitch jested, "Will do Nick. Why get sore feet when you can get saddle sores on the seat of your pants?"

He continued, "I have a couple of wire boys in the Mercyville Station Telegraph Office, so if you don't mind, I'll be lazy and telegraph the station from here." Nick gave him the thumbs up.

Twitch laughed and headed back into the old town hall. As the others headed out the back-garden gate, an upset girl's voice calling out broke the still night air. "Andrew! Andrew Anders! Where do you think you are going? What are you doing in that blue-coat uniform? Did you forget about our dinner date?"

Andy turned and saw Angela in the rose garden by the side of the house with a small picnic basket. "Oh! No! Angela! I'm so sorry I forgot to tell you. I enlisted today, and I'm on duty, and, ah, ah."

Angela pouted, as she started to say, "You're just like a typical male, I never heard of such a lame excuse for missing a …"

Nick came over to her and Andy. "Excuse me. Andy, perhaps you could properly introduce me to your young lady. We meet briefly at the new city hall this morning. However, I was not properly introduced to her, and common courtesies were not observed. I think now would be a good time for these amenities. Andy, would you agree with me?"

Quickly Andy took up the captain's request. "Absolutely sir. Angela this is Captain Nickolas Oldstone."

Andy was now beaming, "Sir, I would like to introduce you to my girlfriend Angela Fishkill-Katz, the most beautiful woman in the world, who I totally adore." Andy blushed seven shades of red as he graciously complimented her.

Nick bowed as he removed his hat and made a broad sweeping gesture with it as he greeted her. "Why, Miss Angela Fishkill-Katz, I do believe in addressing a lady such as yourself most respectfully."

"Why Andy, do we have a southern gentleman here or not?" She added teasingly, "If so, I happen to know a fine young private standing right beside him, who could learn a thing or two about keeping a lady waiting. What do you say, captain?" She suppressed her giggle.

Grinning widely, Oldstone politely flattered her. "I am afraid that I am a Yankee and was born and bred in New England. However, it does not mean that I did not learn my manners."

Clearing his throat, the captain turned to Andy. "I notice Miss Fishkill-Katz has a lovely picnic basket to share with you. Any soldier hates to see good food go to waste, especially when they have not eaten all day."

Winking at Andy, "May I be bold enough to suggest that your duty is, to have that dinner date with Miss Fishkill-Katz? I will have Twitch drop off a horse for you so that you can join us afterward. Do you approve Miss Fishkill-Katz?"

"Oh, absolutely Captain Oldstone. Even if I do say so myself, you're a perfect gentleman too."

Looking at Andy, she teased him. "And some people I know could use a lesson in manners from you, right Andrew?" Smiling from ear to ear, he nodded his head in agreement.

Angela gently elbowed Andy, who saluted the captain. "Right away captain! Ah, I mean Yes sir!" Taking Angela by the arm, they strolled off. "Come on Angela. Let's eat our dinner in the gazebo where we won't be disturbed?"

Happily, Angela whispered to him, "And you can tell me about the heroic adventures you've had today. And I'll tell you what I overheard in the town hall."

Taking a quick look over his shoulder, he tried to see if there were any prying eyes on them. He glimpsed up at the old town hall roof. Annoyed, he scrunched up his face and narrowed his eyebrows and shouted up towards the rooftop. "Twitch get off that roof. I know you're up there. You heard the captain! Get me a horse!"

DIRTY LITTLE SECRETS

Angela was very pleased with the way Andy handled Twitch. She was now more impressed and in love with her man in uniform. She hugged his arm tighter.

As they walked to the gazebo, Andy started to tell Angela about everything that had happened "I think Katz will be getting what he deserves soon, and we will be free of him. Just wait until I tell you what happened tonight over here. You're not going to believe it."

Starry-eyed, Angela smiled, "Let's eat, and then you can tell me all about it."

Andy and Angela were enjoying their rare moment alone in the gazebo. "Angela, even though the roses aren't in bloom yet, it sure is nice sitting here with you in the gazebo. There is just enough half moonlight to see you.

Angela blushed, "I'm glad the moonlight isn't full yet. If my step-father spotted us together, I hate to think what he would do to both of us. He is one of the nastiest, meanest people."

Andy reassured her, "I don't think we have to worry about Katz anymore." Andy then told her about what happened at the old town hall.

She was shocked that she had not heard the gunfire from her home across the street. "Andy, do you think it is safe for me to go home tonight?"

Andy thought, "No, I think you should go straight to the Mercyville Inn and stay with my Aunt Abby."

Angela agreed, "Ok I'll do that," and then she lamented, "I wish my mom and dad hadn't passed away. My mom died of consumption, and my dad died in an accident. I wish they were still alive, and my mom never married Katz."

Andy replied remorsefully, "Yea, my mom died of consumption too. I don't know what happened to my dad either. Some people say consumption took him away, but I don't think so. It's as if everyone in Putnam is afraid to say even two words about him. It's like he never existed. He doesn't even have a tombstone in the cemetery, and I don't know why."

Angela just shook her head not knowing what to say to Andy about his dad. She thought about how consumption was taking so many people these days and causing many complications with couples not knowing whether they were first cousins until long after they married. "Andy, what was your mom's maiden name?"

He had to think about the complicated family relationship for a minute, "My mom's maiden name was Elizabeth Evelyn Everstone, and Katz is her late sister's husband's cousin. I guess with neither of us being true blood relatives to Katz, and even though you are his stepdaughter, it means we're not even blood cousins."

Angela was relieved by Andy's logic and thought about how family ties in New England were often messy and sometimes too complicated to comprehend. She said, "You know I was thinking, Katz doesn't have any children of his own. My mom's dead. So, if something happened to Katz, you don't suppose we would inherit anything do you?"

"Angela, that would be weird! I think it would happen if the moon started to rotate backward around the earth. Even if we did inherit one penny, I get the feeling we would inherit nothing but trouble."

They both looked at each other, and they burst out laughing about inheriting trouble.

Angela, what's your mom's maiden name? I don't remember her much."

"Her name was Laurel as in Mountain Laurel. To be more precise her full name was Matilda Ann Laurel."

"She had a beautiful and sweet name. I've been wondering? Where does your hyphenated name Fishkill-Katz come from?"

Angela grinned, "It's an old New England name, and you'll probably laugh. Even I giggle when I say his name out loud."

"My father's full name was Artemis Millhouse Fishkill." She giggled when she said it.

Andy did not laugh, but he did stop in mid-chew when she said it. "How very odd. I know I've heard that name before in Putnam, but I don't remember where. Maybe they were my mom's neighbors. By chance are you related to them?"

"I don't know. It would be nice if I were, but I don't have any relatives that I know of in Putnam. I guess I really am an orphan."

Both ate silently for a minute or two. "Aunt Abby is not your aunt? You have always called her Aunt Abby."

Andy replied, "That's right we are not related by blood. Aunt Abby was a friend of my mom and dad. When Abby married Cardstacker, she moved down here to Mercyville. Aunt Abby raised me. She is a prim and proper lady. A real sweetheart and she is very smart too. I love her biscuits and books. She has a bookshelf in every room of the inn."

Angela meekly asked him, "Can we talk to your Aunt Abby and find out about the Fishkill family in Putnam and if I'm related to them? I so want a family."

Andy grinned from ear to ear. "Sure, I don't see why not. Ask her when you stay at the inn, tonight."

They heard a couple of horses whinnying as someone led a string of horses up to the gate. A young man's voice called out questioningly, "Is there a private here named Andrew Anders?"

"Hold your horses. I'll be right with you." Andy got up from the gazebo bench and gave Angela a quick kiss on the cheek, "I think I have to go, Angela."

"Not so fast mister." Angela grabbed the front of his coat and pulled Andy to her lips. "There! Now that you've had a real kiss don't forget who gave it to you." Grinning seductively, "Now off you go sweetie pie. And don't forget, when I see you again there will be more of these for you."

Andy grinned and chuckled, "Now that's one order you can give me whenever you want to." Even in the dim moonlight, he could see her cheeks blush a rosy red.

"Come on you two, this isn't lover's lane, is it? I don't have all night." The young private quipped.

"Hold your horses! I'm on my way." Andy grabbed the gate and turned ever so slightly to catch one last glimpse of her, as she peeked out of the gazebo.

"The telegraph message said not to forget to bring the horses. You wouldn't happen to know where Captain Olson is, would you? I got a horse for him too," The confused young rider inquired of Andy.

Taking the reins, Andy mounted up. "Thanks for saddling up the horses, follow me with the string of them since I know the way blindfolded to the captain."

The young man quipped, "Don't put yourself out on my account, if it weren't for the half-moon tonight, we would both be blindfolded." They both laughed.

Angela's heart ached for Andy as she watched him head across the field towards the barns along the north plantation border. She muttered half out loud, "Private Andrew Anders, you're not getting away from me that easily, thinking you can run off with the Union Army. Well, two can play that game, mister."

She hiked up her dress and bolted across the fields toward the newly created Camp Mercyville.

As Andy rode across the unplanted tobacco field, he inquired of his escort, "What's your name and rank?"

"Philo Marshbottom, I think I'm a private? I just finished signing up when they gave me this string of horses to bring to you out here in the dark. I thought it was somewhat odd of you being out here alone in the dark without a horse, but who am I to question Birdy. By the way, what's your name and rank?"

Andy chuckled while thinking is that what I sound like to the captain and the rest of them. He responded, "Private Andy Anders at your service. A pleasure to meet you Private Philo Marshbottom. By the way, the captain's last name is not Olson, its Oldstone."

"Oh, it's a good thing you told me, I'd hate to mess up in the first hour of being a private." They both laughed at each other and became friends.

"I see some lights up ahead by the barns. What's going on up there?" Philo inquired.

"It is very unpleasant business, and we are heading right for it. As soldiers, it's something we are going to have to get used to I fear." Andy hated thinking about who he would find dead and buried in the shallow graves. They could be his friends after all. If so then he would have to get a message somehow back to their families in Ireland and Italy.

Nervously Philo could make out shapes of men gathered together up ahead. They were in the lantern light under a large oak tree over by the barns. Their angry voices carried in the crisp night air, "Andy, there sure is a crowd of angry soldiers up there. It sounds like a lynch mob to me more than anything else. I think they want to string someone up."

Andy listened to the voices of the soldiers and agreed with Philo, "I think your right about that. When murderers kill someone for no reason, they deserve no sympathy. It sounds like the captain has his hands full, wouldn't you agree Philo?"

Philo did not answer, as he felt sick to his stomach at the thought of a lynching. When they got close enough to the crowd of men, Andy said, "Philo, take the horses and put up a tether line between those trees over there out of the way, and guard them until we come back for them. Got it?"

Philo was proud of his new responsibility, without realizing Andy and he was the same age and rank, "Yes sir, Private Andy, sir." Andy dismounted and handed the reins over to Philo, and then he started over to the captain.

That is when he noticed the bodies by the tree, so he changed course toward them. As he came upon them, he could not make out who the corpses were in the darkness under the tree. No one noticed him step back and pick up a lantern from near the pit. He brought it over to the deceased, holding it high over them so he could see their faces.

He sighed and hoped they were not his dead friends. He saw their faces and his hope faded. Sadly, the corpses were his friends.

At first, his stomach turned sour, and then the anger rose within him. Not so much for the murderers, but against the mayor, who must have ordered it just because he did not want to pay them for doing honest work. Andy vowed the mayor would get his due one day, and he would be there to see it. He promised the dead men that he would make sure the mayor ends up on the gallows.

From behind him, he heard the captain's voice, "It's them isn't it?" Andy nodded his head. He did not even think it might be too dark for the captain to see him nod his head. However, his lantern gave off just enough light for the captain to see the back of Andy's head move up and down slowly. "Andy says it's the Irish and Italian craftsmen."

There was a dangerous silence surrounding the crowd of soldiers. It was the silence of anger and not sadness which engulfed all of them. The captain ordered, "Alright men, let's get them into the wagons and take them over to." The captain stopped for a moment when he realized that he didn't know where to take them, so he called out, "Andy, where's there a funeral parlor around here?"

Andy heard his question and choked up swallowing hard before answering, "That would be the Mercyville Funeral Parlor. It's up on the big hill, a block or two from the Mercyville City Hall."

As was his habit, Digger looked around to see where everyone was standing. He spotted one of the recruits talking to Matthews, "Hey, Falsemouth get away from the prisoners!"

Nick ordered, "You all heard Andy. Load their bodies onto Jankowski's wagon and ..." The captain was rudely interrupted before he could finish about gently handling the dead bodies.

The polish teamster, Jankowski objected. "Wait a minute. No dead man is riding in my wagon. It's bad luck. I ain't going to have any of them stinking up my wagon. I learned that in the Great Walk of 1845 to Mexico. I ain't going to smell it in my wagon every time I go to use it. I just ain't."

Unnoticed, Digger walked over to Jankowski giving the little speech and interrupted the teamster just before he finished rattling on about the dead. Digger quickly silenced him.

Jankowski suddenly found himself sitting in the dirt a dozen or so yards from his wagon with the wind knocked out of him. He sat there dazed and not hurt except for his sore tailbone and pride. He was not sure how Digger ever grabbed him so fast and flung him so far while he spoke.

They loaded the remains onto the wagon and Digger looked at Jankowski. "Do you want to get paid for tonight or not? To get paid, drive this team to the Mercyville Funeral Parlor as the captain said. If not, stay out of the way and walk back to the quartermaster's tent with empty pockets and no wagon."

Pouting, the polish teamster climbed up and took his seat as he reined in the horses and slowly led the procession of soldiers back to the station and then over to the Mercyville Funeral Parlor.

The remaining soldiers awaited Nick's next orders, along with what he wanted them to do with the three bound prisoners. Most of the soldiers wanted to lynch the murderers on the spot, but they would respect Nick's decision.

Digger dug into his pocket as he was turning toward Nick and handed over some papers. "Sir, here is the witness statement. I wrote up his very detailed account of the murders and burial. He won't say what he did with the crates, and he will only talk to you about them. Oh, before I forget Ham had these brass slugs on him."

"Oh Thanks, Digger." By lamplight, Nick took a brief look at the slugs and then slipped them into his pocket. Silently he reviewed the documents very carefully. The witness statement made it very clear that the slave traders murdered the Irishmen and Italians, and forced him to bury their bodies.

Digger noticed Private Falsemouth high tailing it between two tobacco barns toward camp. Digger got a gut feeling something was not right about him, so he decided to follow Falsemouth.

As the captain read the witness's account, Ham came over to talk to him. "Captain, sir. I'm sorry there were corpses in the hole. I honestly thought they were crates. Please forgive me, sir. I honestly did not know what the murderous scoundrels had done. I heard shots and came over, and saw them riding away while that feller was filling in the hole. I honestly thought it was the crates he was burying."

Nick looked into Ham's eyes and saw he was sincerely truthful. "It's okay Ham. I need you to give your statement to Digger though."

Nick looked around for Digger but did not see him. "Ham, I'll have Digger get back to you later. If not tonight, stop by my tent in the morning, and I'll have someone take your statement, okay?" Ham shook his head affirmatively.

The one thing that Nick wanted was for someone, anyone, to shed some light on where the crates were. He stepped away from Ham and headed over to the witness by the tobacco-drying barn.

"Guard, I'd like to have a word with our guest under protective custody." The guard moved back a bit but stayed handy just in case they were wrong about the man being an unwilling accomplice and only a witness.

"I'm Captain Oldstone, and according to your statement, you're a Mister Jacob Weedon. Is that correct?"

Jacob slightly bowed his head at the captain's inquiry. "Yes sir, I'm Jacob, and I swear it is all true. I even swore on my small travel Bible for the sergeant that it was all true. I got it in my pocket if you need me to swear again, Captain."

"That won't be necessary. I believe you, son. What are you about nineteen or twenty years old maybe?" The young man shook his head yes.

The captain continued, "Jacob, we found the bodies you buried for the murderers, which made you an unwilling accomplice. Under state law, if I turn you over to the local authorities, which would be the mayor's police force. They would hold you for trial, and if found guilty then you would hang with the others as an accomplice to murder. Jacob, you do realize this, don't you?"

A bit scared, Jacob answered, "I didn't know you were still going to hang me, sir."

"Jacob, I am not planning to hang you. I am trying to figure out a way not to turn you over to the mayor's police force. I get the feeling that if I turned you over to the Mayor, you would be blamed for their deaths and mysteriously die of unnatural causes. Do you get my drift?"

Nervously Jacob nodded his head again, "I think I'm in worse trouble then you think I am. They told me to mind my own business because the judge is in the mayor's back pocket too. That's why I hid the crates."

With this new revelation about the local judge, the captain remained quiet for a minute or two before answering, "No, we're not going to let that happen to you. In fact, you are not being accused of anything. As long as you cooperate with me and do what I tell you to do, I will help you. I have come up with a plan. Moreover, the first thing I am doing is doubling your guards. As soon as you tell me what you did with the crates, we will go get them, and I'll move you to a more secure place, where the mayor can't get you."

"A little bit relieved by the captain's words, Jacob asked him, "And where would that be?"

The captain gave his Old Nick grin, "Why Jacob, have you ever walked through the woods and seen the forest through the trees? Why! I'm going to hide you in plain sight of course."

With these words said, not only was Jacob more concerned about his life expectancy but he doubted the captain's sanity, he still quietly nodded his head in agreement with the madman. All he could think of was the Bible passage about walking through the shadow of the valley of death and not fearing anything. Jacob was afraid, and the Bible passage did not reassure him that he would come out of this alive. As for the captain, Jacob figured you just had to put your faith in the hands of a madman at least once in your life, so he decided to trust the captain. After all, it sounded like a better idea than trusting the mayor and his cronies.

The captain noticed Jacob doing some earnest soul-searching. He remembered seeing his fellow soldiers doing the same thing the night before a battle or just before an attack, so he decided to bide his time a bit with Jacob. "Do you know if there are any other bodies buried around here or not?"

At first, Jacob did not hear him, and then in response, he shook his head no. He thought for a moment, "Oh, I heard them talking about a pauper's graveyard out here somewhere north of the fields, but I couldn't find it."

Nick thought for a moment, and then calmly asked, "While we're on the subject, did you help bury any other bodies?"

Jacob raised his face up and looked the captain in the eyes, "No sir, I buried just those five bodies."

The captain decided to take the chance Jacob would tell him what he really wanted to know, so he chose his words very carefully, "Please explain something to me. If these dead bodies filled in the hole you were digging for the crates from the old town hall, what did you do with the crates? Did you bury them elsewhere? Or did you hide them where they wouldn't look for them?"

The captain could see by Jacob's facial expression that he was thinking how best to answer this question about the crates.

Nick compassionately said, "Jacob, I know you didn't have time to bury the crates here because you didn't have time to dig a new hole before we arrived to seize the property for the Union. I figure the bodies were in the way, so naturally, you probably moved crates to a temporary location because you thought they were going to kill you. Am I right?"

Jacob sighed, "You guessed right sir, I didn't bury them. I hid them really good because if they ever came after me, I needed a bargaining chip."

"That sounds fair enough, but it is now the time for you to tell me where you hid the crates. Well?" The captain knew Jacob was getting up the nerve to tell him the secret about the crates, so the captain decided to wait him out. Therefore, he just stood there trying to be as friendly as possible to Jacob, and waited, and waited until Jacob was ready to talk.

Jacob hesitated for a minute or two, "Ok, I guess you should have them. I think it is better if you get the crates instead of the mayor and his murderous henchmen. I will take you to the crates, but they are a bit of a far walk. We will need two wagons."

The captain's ears perked up, "Hold up a minute, you're right. We need wagons for the crates and more men. Are the crates near the station by chance?"

"No, sir. We pass the station on the way there, but it is a long haul. I had one wagon and had to make two trips."

"Ok, in the morning, we'll get a couple of wagons and get your crates. Thank you, Jacob." The captain called out, "Private Anders, where's my horse?"

The captain could hardly see Andy in the moonlight. Andy pointed to a dark patch of trees a short distance to the east, "Private Philo Marshbottom is looking after them over there."

Philo heard Andy mention his name and even though no one could see him, he snapped to attention. On the other hand, the captain was trying to figure out exactly who this Private Marshbottom was and why had he never heard of him before.

Philo had excellent night sight and could see the captain in the moonlight, "Over here sir." He stepped out of the dark shadows.

The captain could see the recruit in the moonlight, "You're Private Marshbottom, right?" Philo nodded.

The captain could not tell much about him, but he did sound innocent enough. "Alright Philo, we need a wagon, and we're going to wait here for you to get it. Go to the quartermaster tent and bring back a teamster with a wagon."

Philo took his mission to heart, and he snapped to attention as recruits do and saluted. The captain smiled at Philo's enthusiasm and returned the salute.

As he watched Private Philo ride off in the right direction, Jacob inquired. "Ah Captain before we go, are you afraid of ghosts?"

The captain hesitated for a moment before replying, "I'm not very superstitious, and I haven't met a real ghost that's scared me yet. Besides the only ghosts I know of are manmade worries, human frailties and fears from deep in our minds, and not just on the line of battle. I've seen grown men talk themselves into running away from a battle because of fear. Why do you ask?"

Jacob, having second thoughts suggested, "Ah, I'm talking about real ghosts and not human fears. You may not want to go near where I hid them. Captain, with some help from you and some dynamite, we could easily bury the crates forever."

Captain Oldstone thought for a while before answering him, "No Jacob, I swore an oath to protect and preserve the Union. We need to follow through for the greater good and find out what's inside those crates. I get the feeling it really matters."

Jacob nodded his head in full agreement with the captain. "Alright, I will take you. Do you have some paper and an envelope I could use? I need to write something down on it."

Nick grinned and inquired, "Directions to where you buried the crates?"

Jacob nervously replied, "No, I need the paper for my last will and testament. I would be much obliged if you would please witness it for me. The other night, I had a nightmare about something bad happening where I hid those crates. I assure you, nothing good ever comes from my bad dreams."

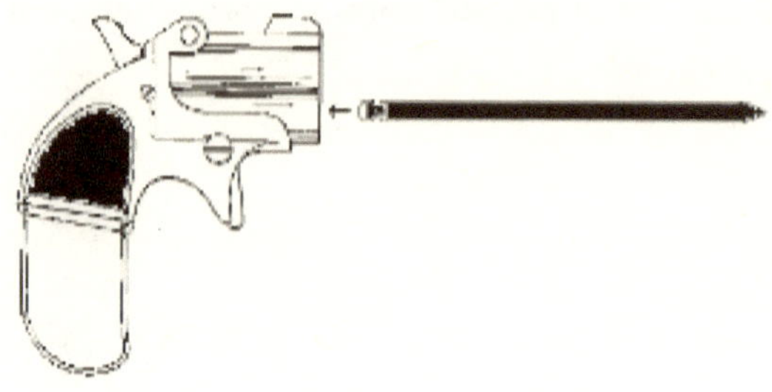

DEADLY LITTLE DARLING

As they waited for Private Marshbottom to bring a wagon, Captain Nickolas Oldstone realized he had not seen Digger since the boys took the corpses to the Mercyville Funeral Parlor. Oldstone wondered if Digger went with them. That's when he remembered that Digger was superstitious and did not like to be in the presence of the dead at night, nor to commune with the dead for any reason.

Oldstone gave a high-pitched whistle and Digger did not answer, so he shouted, "Digger!" He heard Digger's nickname echo as it resounded in all directions, but still no Digger, "That was a stupid thing for me to do." He commented more to himself than to Jacob Weedon or his guards.

He checked his pocket watch, and it was nearly midnight, "Guard, take Mister Weedon back by the drying barn away from the prisoners, and wait there with him until the other wagon arrives."

Angela poked her head around the corner of the barn and nonchalantly started across to the tree where the rest of the soldiers were standing. In their lamplight, it was hard for her to see what they were doing under the large tree. She hoped the stolen private's uniform from the quartermaster's tent would fool them.

While there, she'd had a horrible time finding pants that fit her short legs. Finally, she'd given up and rolled up the bottoms until she could hem them up in the morning. Of course, all the boots were too big for her feet, so she packed the boots full of extra socks. To make her illusion perfect, she stuffed her long red-hair down the back of her coat. However, whenever she moved her head too much, her cap kept popping off. She had to push it back down continually. She figured her long hair was just a minor inconvenience and finally she used her long thin hatpin to keep the cap from falling off completely.

She saw Andy, but at the same moment, Captain Oldstone was heading over to talk to him. She took this opportunity to sneak over to the group of soldiers by the tree.

Once by the great tree, Angela heard a guard say he needed to take a break. Biting her lip and taking a deep breath in anticipation Angela quickly mimicked a young man's deeper voice, "I'll take over your watch while you take your break." Her impersonation worked. No one questioned her.

One of the other young recruits came over to her, "Hi, I'm Private Winslow. Who are you?"

She started to sweat until she realized his voice was almost as high pitched as her own. She quickly replied with her fake young man's voice, but she made a slip of the tongue, "Ah, Private Andy, I mean Sandy! I'm ah, Private Anders, I mean Private Samuel Sanford Sanders. My friends call me Sandy."

To distract him even more, she rapidly kept asking him questions, "Ah, how is guard duty going? Are the prisoners behaving? Ah, do they complain a lot? Have you had your break, yet?"

It worked, soon the rest of the raw recruits were chattering away, and she could stop asking questions. She relaxed and imitated them as they stood around leaning on their muskets. She carefully listened to them talk about the prisoners, and some new game called 'baseball' that included running home.

All this time she kept an eye on Andy. She noticed the captain took Andy aside, away from the prisoners, but she could not hear him say, "Andy, Jacob Weedon, our witness, hid the crates a fair distance off the plantation. We are going to retrieve the crates as soon as a wagon arrives."

The captain whispered, "Its nigh onto midnight and we have been running this to ground most of today. You have performed admirably today. I think you need a good night's sleep. Dismissed. Get some shut-eye. In the morning, I'll fill you in on what we find."

Andy felt let down at being relieved of duty and more or less told to go to his room, or tent in this case.

"Is that an order Captain Oldstone? Because after finding my friends dead like that, I am all wound up, sir. I would rather be allowed to see this through to the end if you don't mind sir."

Surmising this would be Andy's answer, Nick said, "Alright Private Anders, but while you wait, find someplace comfortable to close your eyes until we move out. It looks like Jacob Weedon is taking my advice and getting some shut-eye over there. Why don't you join him? It's about the safest place with the guards over there." Andy nodded, "Yes sir, I'll do just that. Promise to have someone wake me."

Nick teased him, "Andy, I don't make promises I can't keep," He chuckled, "But more importantly, I do not take orders from privates if you get my drift. Now get some shut-eye. That's an order!" Andy obeyed his captain and headed over to the tobacco drying barn to bed down by it for some much-needed rest.

Still undecided about what to do with the three prisoners, Nick headed over to them. He inquired of the first guard he met near the oak tree with the prisoners tied to it, "Private, what's your name and rank?"

CHAPTER EIGHT

The very young and short recruit snapped to attention and nervously stuttered, "Private Samuel Sanford Sanders reporting for duty, sir!"

"Private Sanders, I don't remember you. You're a recruit, right?" Angela nodded her head and almost lost her cap, but pushed it back on straight.

Nick wondered if he ever was that small and raw once. "Ah, Private Sanders are any of the prisoners giving you any trouble?"

Angela started to say something, but she almost messed up her fake voice by squeaking off key. Smartly she cleared her throat and deepened her voice, praying it was enough to fool him. She just wanted to be near Andy, "No sir. They seem to be a very whiny lot of rebel malcontents. They are highly annoying if I dare say so myself. I hope I am not that whiny if I am ever captured and held for ransom or incarcerated as a prisoner during the coming war, sir. I would rather shoot myself and put an end to it, rather than whine as they do. It is downright embarrassing listening to them."

Nick chuckled, "Okay, I get your point. Listen very carefully to what your prisoners whine about and report as accurately as possible about what they say later to Sergeant Palgrave." He continued inquiringly, "You collected their weapons? Was there anything odd or unusual about them?"

Private Sanders responded, "Nothing much. We kept their bullets and gave the soldiers protecting our witness the unloaded handguns, sir."

Impressed by their ingenuity, "Ok, that is a good decision to separate the guns from their bullets. Has anyone checked the prisoners' ropes lately?"

In the lantern light, Nick could barely make out the look of dread that came over the young private's face, "No sir."

Nick smiled slyly and whispered to Private Sanders, "Alright, let's have a bit of fun with these prisoners, shall we?"

Mischievously, in a loud, commanding voice to his recruits, he shouted, "Ah-Ten! Hut!" As his words echoed across the tobacco fields, the guards snapped to attention rather noisily. One young guard even dropped his musket. Angela tried to keep a straight face as she rejoined them in their somewhat straight line.

"Privates, you are all guarding three prisoners, and the whole purpose is to prevent them from escaping or hurting you or anyone else for that matter. It has come to my attention that no one has checked their bindings of late."

The three prisoners were wide-awake and smirked at the recruits. The guards looked at one another questioningly. Nick continued, "Let us learn a valuable lesson here. You two guards will hold your bayoneted muskets at the prisoners, while another guard disarms himself before approaching the prisoners. Approach the prisoners only when you have determined it safe to do so, and one at a time. Remember, do not come between your prisoners and the bayonets as you thoroughly examine their bindings. You will verify in a loud voice whether their bindings are loose or tight, so all of us know the condition of their bindings. Now proceed."

Another young recruit asked the captain, "What if one of the prisoners tries to escape, sir?"

The captain grinned, "Why you either shoot him or bayonet him of course."

To purposely unnerve the prisoners, the captain gave his old Nick grin, and then he coldly and callously commented, "Either way, if you do your job right, I expect the attempted escapee to be dead."

When the prisoners heard this, their eyes seemed to grow as wide as pie plates in the lamplight, except Matthew's eyes, whose eyes narrowed in hatred even more as he sneered.

Nick grinned and kept his hand resting on the Union-issued Colt revolver in his holster to remind Matthews who was in charge here. Nick preferred to be safe than sorry. He kept his Colt ready just in case any of the prisoners tried to take advantage of the young guard checking their bindings.

As the young private was about to bend over to check the bindings, Nick interrupted him, "Private, back off for one moment." He backed off.

Nick directed, "Sanders assist the other private with his examination of the bindings by placing your bayonet under Mister Matthew's chin during the examination."

Angela was unsure what she was supposed to do, "Yes sir! Ah, how close do you want me to get to the prisoner, Captain?"

Nick looked at Sanders for a moment, "If you have been through bayonet practice with Digger or Twitch, you know I mean close enough to shave him with a dull razor." He seriously added, "I want you to get right in his face with your bayonet, Private. Remember, I mean close enough to nick him while shaving, so make it as close as you can get with the tip of your bayonet."

Reminiscing, he spoke loud enough to intimidate the prisoners, "As for me, I would advise you to keep the prisoner off balance by touching their jugular vein with just the very tip of your bayonet."

"Yes, sir." Angela as Private Sanders grinned and did just that to scare the prisoners. Even though Matthews was an angry man, his eyes bugged out the moment she touched the sharp pin-like point of her bayonet to his neck, causing him a great deal of discomfort.

Nick was impressed by Private Sanders handling of the bayonet against Matthews' throat, "Excellent job positioning the bayonet, Private Sanders." Angela grinned from ear to ear and showed her teeth, which scared the prisoners even more.

The captain, suppressing a smile continued, "Gentlemen, you may now proceed. Step one, check their hands for hidden weapons. Step two check their pockets. Again, make sure they are still empty. If not, place the contents into your cap and give it to another guard to give to me. Step three, feel up their bindings make sure the hemp rope is good and tight. That's right, pull on the ropes good and hard, and don't be afraid if they wince or complain. The more they complain that the ropes being too tight, the safer it will be for you and your team."

Under the whale oil lamp light, as a private went through the first prisoner's pockets, he reached inside the prisoner's coat pockets and removed everything he found. The other guard took the stuff and brought it over to the captain.

Nick examined the contents, a notebook, some loose change, a small penknife and a piece of paper balled up into a wad. No pen or pencil though, "Search the prisoner again. He should have a pencil on his person somewhere. I suggest you remove his riding boots and thoroughly look inside each one. I think Matthews is too smug, hand me his riding boots. I bet he has something hidden in them to help him escape later. And don't forget to check the inside of his socks that's right all the way to the tip of the toes."

Matthews kicked at the soldier who was trying to pull off his boot. Momentarily caught off guard Angela pressed the tip of her bayonet even harder against his jugular and this time she drew a few drops of blood. Matthew quickly stopped kicking at the searchers and possibly injuring one of them.

"We found something, sir." The private handed the item over to the other guard, who passed it to the captain along with the pair of boots.

By the lamplight, Nick looked at the oddly capped tube found in the toe of the sock. He realized it was a watertight container. Opening it, Nick saw the end of a note rolled up. He carefully slid out the paper and unrolled it. Interesting enough, all it had on it were numbers. He rolled it back up and resealed it in the tube, and slipped it into his pocket for later examination.

Next, he took the pair of riding boots and started squeezing the sides of each boot. "Private Sanders switch off with Private Winslow. Come over here and do what I do, but to the other boot for me. Closely examine the other boot."

As he pressed the side of a boot, he felt something stiff hidden inside the leather wall of the boot. It was a thin nine-inch ice pick threaded on the blunt end. He waved it at the slave master, "Nice pig sticker you have here, Matthews."

CHAPTER EIGHT

Satisfied there was nothing else in that part of the boot, Nick turned it over to examine the heel and sole. Sure enough, there was something odd about the heel. He took the prisoner's penknife and scrapped the gunk off of the bottom of the heel to reveal two screws. He quickly undid the heel screws with the tip of the pocketknife. Inside the heel was a tiny tube with a small bullet loaded into it.

Angela felt the soft leather of the other boot and found a strip of metal slid into a pocket on the inside wall, "Sir, I found an odd strip of thin unsharpened metal banding notched at both ends. There appears to be a compartment in this heel too. I'll need the pen knife to open it."

Nick willingly obliged and handed Sanders the tiny penknife.

As Angela reached for the penknife, she had a brief panic attack worried if he would notice her nails.

She was so glad she didn't tint them red like the other girls were doing this year, and that she broke a nail the other day and had to clip them shorter than usual. She prayed it was too dark for him to see the reflection off her shiny fingernail polish on her smooth rounded nails.

He passed her the penknife, barely looking at her in the lamplight. "Here you go, Sanders."

She was relieved when he did not notice her nails as he handed her the penknife. She made a quick mental note to cut her fingernails just as short as the young men do.

Upon opening the heel, they were both surprised by the body of a miniature derringer without a barrel in it. Sanders removed it from inside the heel, "Captain, please hand me the tube you found hidden inside the other heel."

Nick handed the tube to Sanders. With a quick click sound, Sanders loaded and snapped the derringer shut. Giving it back to him, the captain commented, "Hmm. It works but is a bit awkward and difficult to hold."

The captain looked at it and noticed two small slots in the short handle, "Sanders, watch and learn something new. Hand me the metal band you found in the leather backing of the boot."

Nick bent the thin band of smooth metal in half, so it formed a crude loop. He then snapped it in place in the slots at the bottom of the derringer to create a crude handle, "There, we have the handle in place. I bet this sharp threaded ice pick screws into this threaded hole under the front of the barrel."

He screwed the nine-inch ice pick into the small threaded hole just below the barrel. "Vicious little weapon, a single shot twenty-two with a small bayonet on the front and a banded metal handle. What won't they think of next?"

The recruits were amazed at the contraption the two of them had assembled. Nick stood there and brought the deadly little darling to bear on Matthews the supposed slave master. Nick aimed the weapon right at his face and saw the hatred in Matthews' eyes. Hatred not just for him and the Union, but for anyone who might get in his way.

"You're no slave master. However, you are the leader of this bunch of spies. If I had to guess, I would say you are nothing more than rebel spies using the mayor as a pawn. I wonder how long you have been in Mercyville and who else you have conned with your deceit and lies?"

Matthews continued to smirk and still preferred to remain silent. Private Winslow pressed the tip of his bayonet slightly harder against the man's neck.

The prisoners had mostly empty pockets, though they did have some loose change and brass coin slugs. One had a harmonica and wad of chewing tobacco. The guard gave those items to the captain.

The guards methodically went through all the prisoner's pockets, and boots and nothing else cropped up, except for a small black book they found inside a hidden pocket in Matthew's jacket sleeve.

Nick, searched through all the belongings. He carefully checked the bookbinding and then held up one page at a time testing each page against the hot glass lantern chimney. However, no writing appeared on the pages, so he pocketed it for further examination later on. His hand brushed against Ham's slugs in his pocket. He took one out, and it was identical to the brass slugs found on the other prisoners. He paused to think and quietly slipped the slugs into his other pocket.

Sanders innocently asked him, "Why were you holding the book pages against the hot lamp chimney?"

Nick thoughtfully smiled and explained to Sanders, "Rebels love lemon juice and not just for drinking. They use it to write secret messages. All you have to do is dip a pen nib in the juice, write it down on paper and then let it dry. When someone wants to read it all they need to do is to heat the paper over a flame, and the lemon juice writing reappears as if by magic, but it isn't magic, it's science."

The captain yawned and checked the time on his pocket watch. It was half past three. He thought about it getting to be daybreak in a couple of hours, so he announced, "Guards pack everything up. When the wagon gets here, we'll load the gear on it and walk the prisoners back to camp."

He knew the wagon and horses would be arriving soon, but he did not like the idea of leaving the prisoners here. They were more experienced than the recruits guarding them and could easily overpower them. Plus, Nick worried about the possibility that Digger would get into trouble or need help.

Sure enough, the wagon came rattling up to them in no time at all, "Alright, load up the wagon!" Nick hollered, and then to Sanders, "Since we'll be moving out shortly, go over to the barn and make sure the guards, along with Andy and Jacob, will be ready to move out."

"Yes, sir." Angela turned and grinned, finally she could see Andy, but she wondered if she could fool him too. Standing right in front of him, she woke him with her fake deep voice, "We're pulling out. The captain wants us all over by the wagon."

To her amazement, Andy and the rest of them obeyed her order without question and headed over to the captain. She was delighted that Andy did it. She fooled him too!

Andy walked over to Nick and said, "It's too dark to be morning, and we're getting ready to leave, huh?"

Nick did not pay attention to Andy. Instead, he was preoccupied with keeping a sharp eye on the prisoners every move. "Andy that's right, I don't think we can do anything else here tonight, so I'm taking everyone back to Camp Mercyville and getting some fresh, experienced guards for our unwanted house guests."

Nick was still holding the deadly little derringer, "Here Andy, take a look at this nasty little thing."

He showed Andy the assembled derringer. "What do you make of it?"

Andy turned it over in his hands, looking at it every which way, "I never saw anything like this before. Who had it?"

"The slave master did. It was disassembled and hidden in the sides of his boots and both heels. What do you think of this deadly little darling?"

Questioningly, Andy tried to understand what was going on. He shook his head in disbelief that such a weapon would exist and inquired of the captain, "Hidden? You don't say. Why would anyone hide something like that in his boot?"

The captain knew the answer, but did not necessarily approve of the underhandedness being employed here, "The only reason I can think of … is Matthews could use this deadly little darling hidden in his boot to kill a guard and escape."

"Hmm, that would make sense, but it is so vicious. I guess some people will do anything these days."

A mule team pulled a wagon up to them, and the teamster spoke loudly, "I hear there is a need for a wagon with four mules here. I'm supposed to see a prima donna impresario called Captain Oldstone. Don't just stand there, go find me this opera lover."

Chuckling, Nick turned towards the dark, rough looking teamster, "Why! I do declare! If it isn't the infamous Mister Isaac T. Johnson, Master of the Mule Empire, and just as stubborn."

Isaac grabbed Nick's hand and pumped it for all it was worth. "Nick it's been too long since we last crossed paths. My freedmen are at your service, sir. And I might add you can trust every single one of my freedmen - all of us fought beside you in Lawrence, Kansas."

"Good, we have a good deal to accomplish here in the next few days, and having them beside me will be comforting. Are they all well-armed?"

Isaac chuckled, "We're armed to the teeth, Nick. Also, Jankowski told me what happened out here, and I do apologize."

Nick thought for a moment, "Can we trust Jankowski?"

Isaac said earnestly, "Absolutely, the Czar of Russia enslaved Jankowski. When his village was wiped out during a pogrom, he was the only one to escape. I assure you, he hates slavers more than I do."

Nick replied, "Fair enough, most people don't know about the repeated enslavement of the poles by the Czar."

Isaac confidently added, "I've already spread the word among my freedmen about Matthews and his slavers. We will gladly make sure no rebel makes off with any of the wagons or mules pulling for you. If you need us for more than that, don't hesitate to ask."

The guards brought the three prisoners over. Nick stopped them from getting into Isaac's wagon. Nick ordered, "No! The prisoners are walking, not riding in this wagon. Jacob, you're riding up front with Isaac."

Turning to Sanders, Nick told him, "You're riding shotgun on the back of the wagon. All I ask is that you aim your bayonet at the prisoners at all times. However, something tells me you would not hesitate to shoot a prisoner's ears off at fifty yards."

Angela took her position on the wagon, as Nick continued, "The rest of you make sure Matthews' hands stay tied behind his back and tether it around his neck like a hangman's noose. Good and tight. Hobble his left leg to the other prisoner's right leg. That's right, wrap the rope around it a couple more times and make sure it's secure and tight. I don't want Matthews to slip out of it."

The other guard asked, "What about the third prisoner here sir? How do you want him tied up?"

Nick replied, "Tie the prisoner's hands just like Mathews behind his back. Let him get used to the feeling of the rope. It will be the last stylish thing he will ever wear before he dies. Oh, and double check Matthews bindings, I want his ropes good and tight."

The rest of the guards walked five to ten paces behind the prisoners, in case a prisoner got loose and made a run for it. As soon as the guards finished tying up the prisoners, the procession started towards camp with Nick and Andy riding ahead of Isaac and Jacob. Andy asked Nick, "Did I miss much while I caught some shut eye, Captain?"

Nick sleepily replied, "Nah, nothing much. Just what I told you about our prisoners and that nasty little pig sticker of a derringer. Back in Washington, the Union armament procurers will love to get their hands on that demented little toy. Oh, and Digger's missing. I'm sure he will turn up, as he always does."

Curious about Twitch, Andy inquired, "Did we hear anything further from Twitch? Is he still at the old town hall?"

"Nothing from Twitch. Knowing how he likes to send telegraph dispatches, I expect when I get back to my tent I will find a pile of dispatches stacked a mile high on my desk from him."

Nick chuckled, "Andy, did I tell you the story of how Twitch got his nickname?"

"Ah … No sir, come to think of it, you didn't. In fact, I don't know Twitch's full name or rank either."

Ignoring Andy's comment, Nick grinned and started telling Andy the story, "We laid siege to the Vera Cruz harbor fortress. Its name eludes me at the moment. Anyway, I was a gunner in the artillery and Twitch drove the munitions wagon for our artillery unit. In particular, he delivered the kegs of black powder for the cannons."

Nick continued his narration, "We were mercilessly bombarding the Mexican fortress, for the longest of time. There was little worry about retaliation because the fortress gunners aimed their massive cannons in the opposite direction. They were protecting the harbor and port entrance. They did not have their guns pointing at our positions along the shoreline.

"Somehow their fortress gunners turned one of their massive cannon around and fired it in our direction just as Twitch was on his way with a wagonload of black powder for our battery emplacement.

"The cannonball missed us by going wide, and it hit a grove of palm trees close behind Twitch. Shattered pieces of palm tree flew in every direction and a hot fragment stuck to the back end of his powder wagon igniting the tailgate. He was guiding the mules over the rocky shore to us, and he was entirely oblivious to his burning powder wagon. He continued on his happy journey bringing the burning powder wagon to us.

Nick continued his story, "If you're smart when you see death coming towards you in the form of a burning powder wagon, you stop firing your cannon and take cover. Most of our battery's men took cover. Some of us feared for his life, including me, so we jumped up and down screaming at him to get away from it.

"However, He could not hear us over the other gun batteries, and just nonchalantly kept coming closer to our position. Twitch did not know what we were doing, and he was only paying attention to crossing over that rocky beach. He was oblivious to the danger he was in until a small powder keg blew up in the very rear of the wagon.

We could see him cringe from the noise of the explosion behind him, and we watched him turn around and see that his wagon was on fire."

Chuckling Nick added, "I never saw anyone jump for his life so fast! The whole wagon blew up sky high in a cloud of blue smoke. We thought he was dead with his body scattered to the four winds. We did not even have time to mourn before we saw him standing before us. He was a soot-covered figure with half his clothes burned off and his hair still smoking. He cursed and screamed at those Mexican gunners."

Nick laughingly wrapped up his story saying, "Twitch was so mad that he began to shake and stutter. He even screamed some choice words as to what the Union Army could do with their black powder wagons. And that Andy is how Twitch got his nickname."

Nick and Andy led the procession back to camp, while Angela rode shotgun and waited for a prisoner to make any break for it, so she could prove what a good shot she was with a musket.

A GRAVE SITUATION

During the night, Twitch ordered his men to run a secure telegraph line from camp to the old town hall. The camp's telegrapher piled up, Twitch's numerous messages on Nick's portable travel desk.

Nick caught about an hour or two of sleep before the sunrise unkindly streamed through the tent flaps awaking him. Once up he never fell back to sleep, so he tied the tent flap open and got to work. He began reading Twitch's lengthy telegraph dispatches sent from the old town hall.

According to Twitch, the four captured telegraphers were less than cooperative. None of the prisoners would open their mouths to explain their presence or who they were. Their silence made it difficult to learn anything at all about the mayor's actions. On searching them, Twitch discovered one of the captured telegraphers had something of interest. Namely, a scrap of paper similar to that found in Matthew's boot heel, and this one also had incorrectly totaled numbers.

As for the rest of the captured telegraphers, nothing came of their searches. It was as if none of the four telegraphers ever existed. None of them had any identification on them, not even a picture or letter from a loved one, and no money or loose change whatsoever.

However, the guard was a small fountain of information, which Twitch detailed in his telegrams. Nick now had a rough idea of the number of rebel spies involved. He still needed to know who all the rebel spies were and when they were going to act.

Too bad none of the other prisoners were willing to spill the beans about Mayor Katz. Nick wondered if the rebels were manipulating Katz and using him as a pawn, or if he was the one leading the rebel spies and conspirators against the Union?

Nick was able to garner enough information that the rebel spies were going to do something very soon in Mercyville, but what?

Andy poked his head into the tent to see the captain, "Morning, sir."

Nick greeted him, "Morning Andy, did you sleep well in your new quarters?"

Grinning Andy replied, "I was too exhausted to know, sir. I am a bit of a light sleeper, and the sun woke me I found the mess tent. The eggs and bacon were good. The biscuits were chewy, but dissolved pretty well in the coffee."

Somewhat worried, Andy added, "I was looking for Digger and Twitch, but their stuff is still packed up in their tents, and no one has seen either of them since last night, sir."

Still reading one of Twitch's dispatches, and without looking up, Nick said, "Twitch is safe and sound and still questioning the mayor's men at the old town hall. There's no new information from him."

Rereading the dispatch, Nick added, "But it worries me that Digger is nowhere to be found. Usually, he turns up by now unless he's in real trouble, which as you have gathered is a common occurrence with him."

Nick's stomach grumbled, he looked up at Andy. "You said you found the Mess tent. How about getting some coffee for us? In fact, bring back a pot of it and some breakfast." Forgetting to salute, Andy scurried out of the tent.

Nick wrote out a message to Twitch and dropped it off at the Camp's Telegraphy Tent. He saw Andy hightailing it back with a tin coffee pot and tin cups and balancing what looked like plates piled high with bacon and eggs, and biscuits. Beaming, Andy announced, "Got your coffee."

Nick thought that with a bit more practice Andy would make an excellent juggler someday. Nick said aloud, "Come on Andy, I'm hungry, join me in my tent."

At the very front of his tent in the cold spring air, the captain set up his folding chairs and small travel table. "Oh good, you brought extra cups and breakfast with the coffee pot." He added, "Twitch will be joining us shortly."

Breakfast was just as Andy described it, and the coffee was still hot. Twitch showed up and grabbed a tin plate and cup. He dug into the food taking a healthy portion and filled his cup with the dark, thick coffee.

Sitting down Twitch asked the captain, "I followed your instructions Nick, and I ordered half a dozen men to guard the place and escort our prisoners to the new stockade. We can rest easy for a while."

Nick smiled, "Thanks, Twitch, you handled the events very well last night. Did you get any sleep at all?"

Twitch replied while yawning, "Just enough, Nick. This hot coffee will sure make all the difference to me this morning. As my Dad once told me, with enough coffee anything is possible. What's next, sir?"

Nick lowered his voice, so only Twitch and Andy could hear him, "I have other business to attend to. So, I need you and Andy to go on a treasure hunt this morning for those missing crates."

Twitch looked somewhat skeptical at Nick, "Now how am I supposed to know where they are?"

Nick replied between bites of food, "You don't. Take Jacob Weedon with you. He hid the crates."

Nick sipped some coffee before continuing, "You'll need a contingent of handpicked men. See Birdy and get our old friend, Isaac. You will need a couple of his wagons to retrieve the crates. You have to get to the crates before the mayor, or the rebel spies get their hands on them. I am sure they want Jacob dead, so keep an eye out for an ambush or sharpshooter."

Twitch finished his first cup of coffee while the captain looked at him expectantly, "Now! Nick. You're asking me to do something before I start on my second cup of coffee that is just not right and you know it."

Nick burst out laughing, "Finish your coffee and breakfast, both of you need to get to work, and if you run into Digger, send him my way, I need him today."

As the captain got up to leave, he sat back down and asked, "Oh before I forget, what was in all those packed up crates in the old town hall?"

Twitch stopped in mid-chew and swallowed a bite of bacon, "Nick, it's kind of strange. I went through all those crates, and they were all filled with paperwork from Katz's paper mill. But here's the weird thing, every invoice and bill of lading that I looked at did not add up right."

The captain thought as he sipped the last of his coffee, "Andy, you said you worked on the mayor's books part-time. Do you know anything about these invoices and bills of lading?"

With his mouth still full of biscuit, Andy shook his head, no. After he swallowed, "No, this is the first I've heard of them. The mayor is very fastidious when it comes to money and insists on his books being kept up to date daily. He was driving Bill Taylor the bookkeeper crazy wanting daily updates."

A private came over and handed Nick a sealed envelope, and then left. Nick opened it and thoughtfully got up, "Excuse me I think I'm about to have a hectic day today. I have to talk to Birdy about some misplaced dynamite. Ah, good luck on your treasure hunt. Ah, make sure every man is well armed. After what happened when we returned to the train station yesterday, I'm expecting more trouble from the mayor and his rebel friends."

Nick turned and quickly left heading toward the quartermaster's tent. With a mouthful of breakfast, Twitch pondered, "Now that's odd Andy, why did the captain just tell us to go see Birdy, if he was already going there?"

Andy shrugged his shoulders as he swallowed another mouthful before answering, "I don't know? Maybe he has other things to arrange there, too. Are you going to finish your bacon?"

Twitch looked askance at Andy, "Of course I am, and my biscuit too. Now pass the coffee so I can soak my biscuit in it. I swear we could use these things for target practice and hit them dead center with every shot for a week without shattering even one of them."

Finishing breakfast, Andy dropped off the plates, tin cups, and utensils at the Mess tent and then followed Twitch over to see Birdy.

By the time they got there, a couple of teamster wagons and other soldiers arrived in front of Birdy's tent. Twitch took the lead on this, "Hey Birdy, are those teamster wagons for us, or are they for the captain?"

Grinning from ear to ear, Birdy responded, "What, you two think you're the only ones needing wagons around here? Well, think again."

Pouting, Twitch replied while rubbing the palms of his hands together, "Birdy, we need a teamster wagon and digging implements, what've you got for us, today?"

Birdy, grinning like a Cheshire cat about to pounce on a mouse, "Guys, I could continue to give you a hard time, but the truth is Nick stopped by on another matter, and then placed a couple of camp supply orders, and your order is out back. Follow me." He raised the rear tent flap, and the two followed him out back.

CHAPTER NINE

As Birdy stepped outside, he rambled on, "Now Twitch, don't let this little surprise go to your head. It was entirely Nick's doing, and I assure you he was very explicit in what he ordered for you both. He even threw in two wagons with teamsters, picks and shovels, and two dozen whale oil lanterns in your order. Not to mention enough hardtack for a meal or two on the road for all of you."

And then Birdy whispered into Twitch's ear, "Nick doesn't want anyone to know that I got the first shipment of the new Spencer rifles. So, I gave one to Isaac to hold onto for you, just in case. He's got it in his wagon with a couple of Colt revolvers and ammo. Nick said to use it only if you have to, Okay?"

Twitch said nothing. He'd heard of the Spencer rifle's firepower, and that it could fire ten shots in the time it took to load and fire a musket.

Next Birdy stepped forward, bowed and waved his arm like a circus master or magician would do. He proudly exclaimed to Twitch, "Well, what do you think! Isn't this a grand expedition, I outfitted it myself for you?"

Sure enough, in front of Twitch stood two fully equipped mule team wagons along with two dozen recruits awaiting Twitch's orders. Jacob Weedon sat next to Isaac Johnson all prim and proper in the teamster's first wagon. The rest were raw recruits eagerly waiting to embark on their first march as if going to some far off distant land.

Twitch and Andy looked at each other and burst out laughing because this was a lock-and-load mission all set up for them. When they finally stopped laughing Twitch took command, "Andy, do you believe it! He even arranged for a couple of horses for us." Still grinning, Andy nodded in agreement.

They both noticed that as soon as the recruits spotted Birdy, all of them snapped to attention in formation. Each recruit was well-armed with a freshly cleaned musket with bayonet and carried an extra ammo pouch.

Birdy looked at the recruits and wagons, and he grinned as he spoke to them, "Gentlemen, I turn you over to Lieutenant Twitch to command you. Good luck and good hunting."

Winking at Twitch, Birdy added, "They're all yours Twitch." And then he disappeared back into his Quartermaster tent.

Twitch and Andy mounted the horses. Twitch gave the order, "Isaac and Jacob you're in the lead here, and we will follow, but it sure would help us, Jacob, if you told us where we are going?"

Grinning, Jacob turned and whispered some directions into the ear of Isaac, the lead teamster, who loudly proclaimed, "Follow us to our grave, and you will find what you're looking for."

His wagon lurched forward, and the grand expedition rolled out of camp heading south. Angela, not wanting to be discovered in her role as Private Sanders, brought up the rear. As the recruits marched out the main gate, no one noticed Falsemouth snuck into the ranks too.

The recruits were in good spirits as they marched through Mercyville. Winslow asked Sanders if they could sing while marching. Sanders hightailed it up to Twitch. In her fake masculine voice, she asked, "Sir is it alright if the men sing while we march through town?"

Twitch quickly decided it would be an excellent way to let the townsfolk know they were friendly. "Hmm, it just might be a good idea to do that. Sanders, what are they going to sing?"

Sanders quickly explained, "Winslow's cousin works in a print shop in Charlestown, Massachusetts, and he sent Winslow a copy of some new sheet music. The men heard him singing it yesterday, and they all liked it and learned it. It's called John Brown's Body."

Twitch liked the sound of its name and smiled, "I'd like to hear that new song, but they have to stop singing once we're through town. Permission granted."

"Thank you, sir." Sanders returned to the men to spread the good news.

Winslow who knew the song by heart started off singing it, "John Brown's body lies a moldering in the grave, John Brown's body lies a moldering in the …"

A GRAVE SITUATION

Everyone quickly joined in. At first, they sounded off key, however, they more or less harmonized:

John Brown's body lies a moldering in the grave,

John Brown's body lies a moldering in the grave,

John Brown's body lies a moldering in the grave,

Glory Hally, Hallelujah! Glory Hally, Hallelujah! Glory Hally,
  Hallelujah!

His soul's marching on!

He's gone to be a soldier in the army of the Lord,

He's gone to be a soldier in the army of the Lord,

He's gone to be a soldier in the army of the Lord,

His soul's marching on!

Glory Hally, Hallelujah! Glory Hally, Hallelujah! Glory Hally,
  Hallelujah!

His soul's marching on!

John Brown's knapsack is strapped upon his back -

John Brown's knapsack is strapped upon his back -

John Brown's knapsack is strapped upon his back -

His soul's marching on!

Glory Hally, Hallelujah! Glory Hally, Hallelujah! Glory Hally,
  Hallelujah!

His soul's marching on!

His pet lambs will meet him on the way -

His pet lambs will meet him on the way -

His pet lambs will meet him on the way -

Glory Hally, Hallelujah! Glory Hally, Hallelujah! Glory Hally,
  Hallelujah!

CHAPTER NINE

They go marching on!

They will hang Jeff Davis to a tree!

They will hang Jeff Davis to a tree!

They will hang Jeff Davis to a tree!

Glory Hally, Hallelujah! Glory Hally, Hallelujah! Glory Hally,
  Hallelujah!

As they march along!

Now three rousing cheers for the Union!

Now three rousing cheers for the Union!

Now three rousing cheers for the Union!

As we are marching along!

Glory Hally, Hallelujah! Glory Hally, Hallelujah! Glory Hally,
Hallelujah!

Hip, Hip, Hip, Hurrah!

As soon as the expedition marched past the Mercyville Station, they turned west for a block or two and headed south toward Cemetery Ridge Road.

Andy excitedly blurted out, "See, I told you Twitch, Jacob hid the crates in the old cemetery on the hill."

Twitch becoming a bit preoccupied with keeping a sharp lookout for ambushers did not respond to Andy. When they reached Cemetery Ridge Road, he signaled the recruits to stop singing.

Cemetery Ridge Road was a steep climb for the wagons and taxed the wagon's mule team strength. When they reached the cemetery near the ridge, the teamsters pulled up to rest the teams. Twitch rode up to Jacob in the lead wagon, "Alright Jacob we're here. Now, in which grave did you bury the crates?"

Jacob grinned, "Guess again. Isaac is only resting his mules. We still have a mile or two to go."

Jacob's grin turned a bit sheepish and whispered to Twitch, "I can't tell you because the captain told me not to tell you or anyone else until we arrived there. He said if I told anyone, it would be too dangerous for me. He believes at least one of these recruits is a rebel conspirator, who might try tip off the rebel spies to stop us. However, he also said you would know best how to protect me."

Disappointed, Twitch was about to look at his pocket watch when he heard the Mercyville City Hall Clock Tower chime nine times.

Isaac announced, "We're taking a break for the mules to rest up a bit until they are ready to continue. It will not be long, so do not go far. We'll pull out again in a little while on our journey of adventure."

Twitch pointed at Sanders and Winslow and said, "You two guard Jacob. Protect him, In other words, do not let anyone near him until we're ready to go."

Jacob inquired, "Twitch, is it alright if I visit my family plot? I'd like to see my Granddads' grave."

Twitch gave a thumb's up to Jacob's guards that it was alright. Sanders and Winslow followed Jacob towards some nearby gravestones and markers in the cemetery.

Twitch joined Andy in the cemetery, "Andy, this woman's tombstone is dated 1672. I didn't know Mercyville was that old."

Andy took a good look at the tombstone, "Oh yeah, ah, this part of the cemetery is Jacob's family plot. His family is one of the founding families. They arrived with Thomas Hooker who founded Hartford that year. The Town, Mercyville, wasn't officially established until ten years later in 1682."

Andy noticed that Jacob and his guards were standing near a stone sarcophagus with an odd-looking contraption on top of its cover. Nudging Twitch with his elbow, Andy said, "Hey Twitch, there's something you don't see every day. Take a look at the stone sarcophagus with a bell on it over by Jacob."

Jacob proudly explained, "This flat granite cover is my mom's brother Uncle Bartleby's grave. He was afraid of being buried alive. So, he ordered a reanimation bell installed in the lid just in case he woke up from the dead. Too bad he never got a chance to use it."

Andy's curiosity got the better of him, "Why? Is he still alive?"

"No, he died in 1850 while he was traveling on his way to Chicago on business. He was lost on Lake Erie when the passenger Steam Ship G. P. Griffith burned and sank. We never did recover his body. It's all there right on the lid if you want to read about him."

Out of curiosity, Andy read the writing on the stone lid:

In Loving Memory of

Bartleby Seymour Braxton

Born June 18, 1812

Died June 17, 1850

He died and did not recover from it

when the Steam Ship G. P. Griffith

burned and sank to the bottom of

Lake Erie and took him along with it

May He Rest in Peace with the Fish

Twitch did not hear the whole story about Jacob's uncle. He came over and bent down to look at the bell on the stone, "Well, I'll be. What's that bell and hole in the lid for, Jacob?"

Jacob replied, "It's one of those Reanimation Coffins. You know, in case they accidentally bury you alive. If you wake up inside, then you pull the bell wire and pray someone hears you and lets you out. There's nobody in it, and he was sort of lost at sea, in a lake."

Twitch knelt down to examine the small bell and wire more closely. He flicked the bell with a finger like what you do to a fly off your arm, and the bell dinged once, "Now I've seen everything."

Kneeling there, he thought about it for a minute, "I don't think I'll need one, I'll probably be shot, or run through by a rebel saber in this here war that's coming. Yah, I want a glorious death."

As he started to get up, the Reanimation Bell startled him as it began to ring wildly as if someone dead inside really wanted to get out. Twitch and Andy both jumped back and looked at each other. Andy frantically cried out, "I ain't going to open it! What if it's a ghoul come back to life!"

Excitedly Jacob started screaming and hollering at Andy and Twitch, "Quick get the lid off! They must have dredged his body up from the lake and stuck him in there, and did not tell me! Come on! Hurry up! Get that lid off him!"

Twitch, caught his breath as he tried to shift the stone lid off of the sarcophagus, "Andy, help me! There's some poor devil stuck in there! We have to get him out!"

The bell continued to ring as they both pushed on the sarcophagus cover, but the lid would not budge. When Falsemouth saw Jacob and Twitch trying to push the cover off, he quietly made his way out of the cemetery and back to the rear of the wagons. He wanted no part in moving that lid.

Twitch stood up, ordered two soldiers to help, but they were not strong enough, and Twitch still needed more men to budge the lid. As the bell continued to ring wildly,

Twitch whistled a high pitch whistle and waved at the other soldiers, and he screamed, "Get over here! Now! That's an order!" They came running.

Angela joined the soldiers pushing and pulling on the sarcophagus lid, and it finally started to budge. At first, a small opening appeared between the cover and the sarcophagus base. As soon as it slid aside just wide enough, a hand reached out from inside and grabbed the nearest coat sleeve. Angela screamed and pulled back her arm and fell backward in fear from the granite sarcophagus. Once the lid was off, Private Winslow passed out when the corpse inside sat up.

Faster than you could flip a coin and say heads, Jacob's excitement turned to shock and dismay. He blurted out, "You're not my Uncle Bartleby! What are you doing in his coffin? Where's my Uncle?"

Digger sat up gasping for air, and barely able to hoarsely talk, "Thanks, guys, you are lifesavers, I thought I was a goner for sure."

Everyone was stunned and just looked at each other, trying to figure out, if Digger was raised from the dead or saved from being buried alive. Most quickly figured out, either way, it was a good thing for Digger, he seemed to be alive and not a ghoul.

Twitch demanded, "Quick! Someone get me a drink for Digger! I'll take anything you got: brandy, hard cider, even water!"

Hearing this plea, Isaac, pulled out his flask and handed Digger his half-full flask of hard cider, "Here Digger, take a nip of my private stock, and you'll feel better."

Digger took it, and desperately emptied the contents in his mouth. He chugged it until it was empty. Wiping his mouth with this sleeve, he gasped, "Thanks, I owe you a fifth of the good stuff when we get back. Everyone, tonight the drinks are on me."

Andy offered his hand to help Digger out of his premature grave, "Here Digger take my hand. Can you stand?"

A couple of soldiers gently pushed Andy aside, "Excuse us, Andy, we'll take it from here." They reached down, each one grabbed Digger under the armpits and gently pulled him out of the coffin. They stood Digger up, "Thanks, I'm just a bit sore and stiff, that's all."

He tried to stand on his own, but his knees buckled a little bit. They leaned him against a nearby tombstone for support. They stayed near him until his blood flow got going inside his legs again.

They waited a few minutes for Digger to recover when Twitch ordered, "Help him to the second wagon, so he can ride on it. Digger, you do not have to say anything right now. When you feel better, or we get back you can tell us all about what happened last night." Digger still feeling cramped and wobbly just nodded his head yes.

Twitch looked down at the open sarcophagus, "Hey a couple of you come back here. Let's close this tomb up before someone falls into it and breaks his neck or worse an ankle."

Andy questioned his logic, "Twitch, I think you have your priorities mixed up there. Don't you mean to break our ankle or worse our neck?"

"No, Andy, I said what I meant. When you break your neck, all we do is slide the granite lid over you, and we're done. However, if you break your ankle, we have to lug you all the way back to the camp hospital for the surgeon to examine you. The surgeon will surely cut off your leg, and the rest of your life you'll wish you had broken your neck instead."

Andy, thought about what Twitch said, and somehow it seemed to make sense, or did it?

Andy stepped over to Digger, whispering to him, "How'd you get in there?" Digger whispered back, "Keep your eye on Private Falsemouth. He's not to be trusted. I think he intentionally led me into a rebel trap last night."

"Thanks, Digger, I didn't notice him along with us this morning. I'll tell Twitch, and we'll take care of him when we get back." Digger agreed.

Andy decided to wait for Digger to recover enough before he talked to him again about his premature burial. He wanted to hear the full story from Digger about how much the mayor was involved, and what role Falsemouth played in all of this.

Falsemouth spotted the two talking. He Assumed Digger told Andy about him leading Digger into a trap. He worried that they would come after him, so he slipped away into the woods across from the cemetery.

While waiting to leave, Andy silently worried about what other nasty little surprises the rebel spies planned for them along the wagon trail. He quietly ruminated on this, but soon his mind turned to Angela and how much he missed seeing her this morning.

SURPRISE ATTACK

Jacob led the expedition out of the cemetery and back onto the road. He still didn't tell Twitch where they were going. As they rode on, Twitch's mind was elsewhere. Andy heard Twitch mutter under his breath, "We sure live in a sick world these days."

Twitch had trouble believing anyone could be so callous and sadistic as to bury another person alive. He knew Digger's rescue or reincarnation at the cemetery was not supernatural, but later on, this could lead to trouble for those under his command.

On the far side of the hill the road began to narrow somewhat and started to break up into even narrower wagon ruts. The wagon track was barely wide enough for one wagon to get through at a time. The sides of the wagons brushed against old overgrown blackberry brambles just starting to sprout leaves in the chilly New England spring air.

Isaac, reined in his mules and stopped the advance, "Jacob, if this so-called road closes up anymore, the mules can be stubborn, and they don't like getting stuck in the sides by any of this thorny overgrowth. Is there any other way to get there?"

Jacob smiled, "This is the narrowest part. Around the next bend, you take a right at the fork, and in a mile or so we'll be there."

Twitch overheard their short conversation, and chimed in, "Jacob, I don't like this narrow wagon path. It is ripe for an ambush. Can you tell if anyone has been here since you hid the crates?"

Without hesitating, Jacob replied, "Twitch, I'll know as soon as we get to the next split in the wagon path." Twitch was pleased to hear Jacob was thinking ahead when he hid the crates.

As they rounded the next bend, they came up to the split in the wagon path. The left branch looked like it was traveled more than the right wagon path, which was somewhat overgrown but still passable.

Jacob nudged Isaac to stop and signaled the expedition to stop. Quietly Jacob climbed down from the wagon and said, "We need to check the harnesses because there is a steep incline up ahead. Andy, can you give me a hand here?"

Andy dismounted and made his way between the brambles and wagon to help Jacob. When Andy got there, Jacob pretended to adjust the mule team harnesses as he quickly whispered to Andy, "Let Twitch know there might be a trap up ahead. Yesterday, I left a large oak log blocking the right path. Someone moved the log aside."

Jacob added a little bit louder, "Andy, what you forgot your knife. Well, borrow a knife from Twitch, I'm sure he has an extra knife." Andy understood that Jacob was play-acting, and so Andy headed back toward Twitch.

Twitch was already holding a knife out for Andy to use. As Andy took it, he whispered to Twitch that Jacob noticed the missing log. In a loud voice, "Thanks, Twitch, we'll just be a few more minutes with the harnesses."

Twitch continued the charade, "Thank you, Private Anders."

A bit louder Twitch ordered, "Dismount! We are taking a break right here. Riders check your saddle straps. Infantry check your backpacks."

Once Twitch quietly dismounted, he told Sanders to pass the word to everyone that it was time to get ready for a fight. He gathered a few of the new Mercyville recruits, "There may be an ambush up ahead. Without raising your hand or saying a word, I need those of you who know these woods to slip away up the right wagon track and outflank the track through the woods on both sides. Eyes only, do not engage, unless you are attacked. You are a scouting party. Now get going. Remember, be invisible and quick about it."

He turned away and thought of something else to tell the recruits, but when he turned back, they were all gone. He looked at Sanders, "Dang, I must be getting old! I didn't even hear them sneak off into the woods." Angela smiled, she thought he was funny.

Twitch thought for a moment, and then whispered to her, "Sanders, as a distraction order the remaining riders to keep their horses on the outside for cover and to pretend to be busily fixing each other's saddles and saddlebags."

Soon the scouts began to report in, one at a time. They all reported it was all clear for a couple of hundred yards past the split in the road, but one scout remained out.

Everyone was getting antsy waiting and wanted to move on, but Twitch decided to stall with an impromptu fake inspection and ordered all of them to line up in the middle of the road, at attention.

Just as Twitch was finishing up, there was a rustling near the back of the troops, and a scout out of breath stumbled out of the hedges.

Still out of breath from running back, the scout gasped heavily, "Private Johnston, reporting sir. All clear for a mile on the right flank. However, just past a mile, there are seven shooters on a slight rise hiding behind a stone wall on the right side of the wagon path. And I spotted five more on the left side of the wagon path hiding in the saplings in a maple grove."

Pausing to take a breath, he added, "And I have never seen such long rifles in all my life."

Twitch grinned, "Now that's a scouting report, you can all learn from, thank you for the excellent report, Private Johnston. Wait here while I consult with Sergeant Palgrave. Sanders follow me."

Twitch and Sanders stepped over to Digger, "Are you up for a fight? If so, which half do you want? I think they must be the rebel spies who jumped you and buried you alive. What do you think? It's your call this time."

Digger was quieter than usual. However, Twitch did not see exhaustion from a night in a grave or fear in his eyes. Instead, he saw cold, heartless anger in Digger's eyes.

Digger spoke very quietly, "Today, I think seven to one is better odds than five to one for me if you know what I mean." Sanders kept quiet, not quite getting Diggers math or meaning.

 Twitch understood, "Digger, I know what you mean, but we have to think of the bigger picture of what is going on here. I know you are capable of taking that many down by yourself. However, we need some left alive for Nick to get some answers. He seems to think these rebels are really up to no good, and not just in Mercyville but elsewhere in

New England. We need as many as possible left alive and willing to talk."

Digger looked at him, "Twitch, I overheard enough to know for sure that they are rebel spies. I overheard them bragging about how one rebel is worth ten northerners, and I overheard a lot more before seven of them forced me into that stone coffin and laughed at me. No one laughs at me. Twitch, I need your big Bowie knife."

Angela was appalled by the violent act perpetrated on Digger and the murders of the five innocent dead men buried under the tree. However, she realized there was no way to avoid the violence. She accepted the fact that these rebel spies already had set up an ambush. Digger and Twitch were being forced to act against the rebel force, or everyone in this expedition would all be killed by the spies.

Twitch reasoned it was useless to rationalize with Digger. Twitch stepped over to his horse and pulled out a couple of things from his saddlebags, and said. "We will split the force into three bodies. Digger attack the rebels behind the stone wall with your troopers, and I'll attack the maple grove with my troops. We will leave the main body of troops here, to use the wagons for cover. The recruits trust Sanders and seem to follow him willingly." Digger nodded in agreement.

Twitch continued, "Here you go, Digger. Take both my knives and my spare colt revolver. Remember, I need you to outflank the rebels behind the stone wall with your six recruits backing you up, and I will take my recruits to outflank the rebels in the maple grove. Sanders, you get the remaining twelve recruits to defend the wagons. Is it a deal?"

Twitch put out his hand to shake on it, Sanders stood on her tiptoes, and her small hand joined in on the handshake. Twitch and Sanders went up front to tell Isaac, Andy, and Jacob the plan. Twitch briefly thought about taking the Spencer rifle, but the rifle might be unwieldy with all the saplings in the woods. So, he decided using a Colt revolver was a better choice for hand to hand fighting between these young trees and in the thick underbrush.

Twitch gathered them together and said, "Jacob, the rebel spies will be looking for you. I need your help to distract them up the road."

Twitch explained, "Isaac your orders are to move the wagons very slowly up this wagon track for about a mile where you see a slight rise. On top of it is the stone wall. Across from it is a grove of maple saplings. Do not pass between or stop in front of the stone wall or that maple grove."

Jacob chimed in, "Don't worry Isaac, I'll show you the perfect spot to stop the lead wagon." Isaac nodded his head.

Twitch continued, "Good, Jacob fake a break down at a safe distance short of the stonewall. I need you to lure the rebel ambushers out, and this will be our signal to attack."

Andy asked, "Twitch what do you need me to do?"

Twitch quickly replied, "Andy! Birdy placed a spare revolver under the seat in the second wagon, get it and ride in the second wagon. When the lead wagon stops, you are to get in front of it as fast as you can. I expect at most one, or two rebels might get through to kill Jacob. Stop any rebel ambusher who escapes our trap and attacks you. Sanders lead the recruits to help defend the wagons."

Sanders asked, "What do I do?"

Twitch carefully explained, "Sanders, in case some of the rebel ambushers escape us, you and your recruits are the last line of defense against a rebel charge. Line the recruits up in two rows behind the wagons and be ready to open fire. Can you do that?"

Angela nodded her head yes, "Do you mean line up the recruits like a firing squad? Six to a row?"

"Yes, that is a good way to put it." Then Twitch quickly demanded, "Any more questions? Alright! let's get moving."

The two forces led by Digger and Twitch ducked into the woods on either side of the track. They kept up a fast pace moving quickly through the woods to outflank the rebel trap.

Angela as Sanders gathered the remaining troops around her, and in a fake deep voice, "Our orders are to advance along the wagon tracks and lure the rebel ambushers out from their hiding places and to protect the wagons. If any rebels escape and attack us, we will cut their escape off and return fire."

Winslow asked, "Do we fix bayonets too?"

Thinking quickly, Angela replied in a deep voice as Sanders, "No, we have to wait until we hear the fighting commence. That is when we fix bayonets and line up behind the wagons in two rows, just as my Grandfather was taught to do by George Washington at the Valley Forge camp. Now check your powder and flint, and be on the ready in case the rebel spies change their plan and attack early."

Jacob sat nervously in the lead wagon with Isaac as they headed straight for the rebel trap. Jacob knew approximately where the stone wall was. He just had to make sure that Isaac pulled the wagon up short of the stone wall and maple grove. Jacob had to entice the rebel spies to attack them while staying out of Digger's and Twitch's crossfire.

The expedition took the right fork following Jacob and Isaac into the trap. They slowly inched along the narrow wagon trail. The wagon teams needed to move slowly, in order, to give Digger and Twitch time to get their forces into place, so the rebels' ambush would backfire.

About halfway there, Digger halted his men. "Alright lads, I have a few words to say before we get there. These same men buried me alive. They gave me no quarter, no break.

They wanted me to suffer before I died. They are not your southern gentlemen. They are without honor. They are cold-blooded, sadistic killers. Expect no mercy or quarter from them. So, for us, it's kill or be killed."

Digger paused for a moment before continuing his instructions to the recruits about the enemy, "I know I am asking a lot of you. None of you have ever been in a battle yet, and none of you have killed a man yet. We will sneak up behind them, and you will give me cover. Aim your loaded muskets at them just like you would at a hungry fox, wolf, or bear. You have all hunted before so aim true at their heart. If they see us coming, they will aim at our chests to kill us. If you aim anywhere else, you will miss, and you will be killed, instead of one of them being killed."

He finished up his speech with, "We have one chance at surprise. Remember, you're all giving me cover so make every shot count. I've said enough. Let's get them before they get us!"

In the meantime, Twitch stopped with his men about halfway there, "Men, we are going into a desperate battle. Rebel spies are waiting for our arrival on the wagon track. They do not know we know. We have five targets hiding behind trees with Kentucky long rifles."

He paused and then continued, "We will see them before they see us. We will come up behind them. The trees will be between our targets and us. Our thin and scraggly New England trees will give us the advantage because our rifle barrels are short, and not like the rebel long rifles. We will be aiming at the enemy long before they can turn and fire at us. Their long guns will become entangled with our saplings.

"Take your time, aim true. Make sure you aim at their heart. I will be alongside you and will lead you in this, your first battle. We need to capture at least one rebel spy alive for questioning. If he is wounded, that is okay. That is my mission. Your mission is to give me cover fire. Now before we continue, let us pray …"

Falsemouth ran well ahead of the expedition through the woods to warn the rebel spies that the Union soldiers were on their way. As he ran up to their position, in his excitement, he forgot to give the password. As a result, the first ambusher that Falsemouth ran into thought he was a Union scout. He hit Falsemouth so hard it broke his nose and knocked him unconscious before he could say a word.

After knocking Falsemouth out, the rebel spy recognized him as one of the mayor's men. He figured Falsemouth really should have known better than to have surprised him like that.

Isaac and Jacob took their sweet time getting to the ambush site. Through the trees, Jacob could see up ahead the stone wall on the rise. Putting his hand up, he signaled both wagons to rein in their mules and stop. Jacob played his part as bait very well. He was a bit nervous with a dry throat and sounded hoarse to boot. He was still able to talk loud enough for his voice to carry beyond the stone wall to distract the rebel ambushers.

He started to say, "Hold up here. Our harness came loose again, so we had better see to the harnesses before one slips off and …"

A volley of musket shots from the woods behind the rebel ambushers cut short his impromptu speech. Andy, Jacob, and the teamsters all dove off their wagons for ground cover. A second volley and then surprisingly a third volley echoed through the woods. Finally, all was silent from the wall and woods surrounding the wagon track up ahead.

Angela, disguising her voice as Sanders, took a deep breath, and nervously exclaimed, "Quick men! Line up behind the wagons! That's right! Form two lines of six like I showed you." She glanced at the clouds of blue smoke in the distance. "Fix bayonets! Check your powder! Get Ready!" Nervously the twelve recruits followed Sanders orders.

Andy poked his head up from behind a log by the wagon track. Up ahead from the ambush, he saw clouds of billowing blue smoke traveling fast on the breeze towards them. The billowing smoke was too dense to see through and to know for sure who might be coming their way.

Even though Andy was scared, he tightly grasped the pistol grip and instinctively pulled back the hammer and raised the revolver. He nervously held it pointing at the oncoming cloud of smoke. Perhaps Andy did it for comfort or maybe tried to hide behind the weapon. He did not know why he raised the revolver when he did, Andy just did. Andy felt strange as if watching someone else aim the Colt revolver at the approaching blue cloud. He did not know why. He just knew he had to point it at the approaching blue cloud.

Jacob stood up almost directly in front of Andy, getting in his way just as the blue smoke reached them. Andy could barely make out an outline coming through the acrid smelling smoke. It was a man charging straight at them, but Andy could not tell if it was friend or foe.

Behind the wagons, Sanders and the recruits could not see the running man through the smoke, but they were anxiously waiting to defend. Sanders ordered, "Raise your weapons. Aim at the blue smoke."

The smoky blue cloud dissipated just enough for Andy to make out a running figure almost on top of Jacob. At the last moment, Andy realized it was a bearded stranger with a long-barreled rifle in one hand, and a hatchet in the other, charging straight at Jacob.

Startled by the sight of the charging man, Jacob froze to the spot unable to move. The bearded man wielding the hatchet was about to strike a killing blow at Jacob. Instinctively Andy pulled the revolver's trigger. It fired a single shot over Jacob's shoulder. Jacob screamed from the pain of the powder burn on his neck and the deafening roar of the colt revolver ringing in his ear.

Directly in front of Andy, Jacob started to collapse in pain just as the bearded man's limp dead body bowled Jacob over. Jacob landed on his back on top of Andy, who landed on his back on the ground still grasping the revolver. The bearded dead man pinned both of them down.

Out of the blue smoke, three more rebels appeared as they charged the wagons. The last thing those rebel spies heard was a woman's voice hoarsely screaming at the top of her lungs, "FIRE!"

Nervously the recruits focused on aiming and squeezing their triggers, and not on who screamed the order to fire. The explosive sounds of the recruits' muskets were deafening. With all their ears ringing, Sanders scared and nervous yelled, "Reload! Reload! Quick get ready for another attack! Hold your positions!"

The recruits nervously fumbled with their powder and percussion caps while reloading their muskets. They still managed to get it done. One by one, they aimed. Just as their smoke cleared from around the wagons, they were ready for another onslaught. All the recruits held their positions with raised muskets and fixed bayonets awaiting another assault. But it didn't happen and feeling relieved Sanders ordered her men, "At ease men."

Private Winslow and a few other recruits threw up. Some recruits shakily leaned on the wagon for support while others with tears in their eyes counted their blessings that they were still alive. Angela's stomach was turning, and she felt a bit shaky because she had seen Andy bowled over and she was scared he might be dead.

Isaac went over and rolled the dead man off Jacob and Andy, "Yep, he's dead alright. He shot in the face. In all my years, I ain't never seen anyone getting bowled over by a dead man before. Here take my hand. Are you boys alright?"

Taking a quick glimpse at his mules, "We're in luck! None of my mules got shot, but I can't say the same for the dead rebels up here."

Sanders sent four recruits out to check the three dead rebel spies. "Remember from last night to act as a team, and to place your bayonet on the jugular, until you determine that he is not playing dead. Do not move onto the next body until you have confirmed he is indeed deceased, otherwise, use your bayonet to keep him at bay."

Isaac checked on Andy and Jacob. Both were lucky - they only had the wind knocked out of them from being bowled over by the force of the rebel's attack. They were so unnerved that neither was able to say anything or even to thank the teamsters or Sanders accompanied by the recruits for their help.

Angela felt bad for Andy, who was just standing there gripping the revolver in his hand looking up the wagon track for more blue smoke. For the time being, disguised as Sanders, there was nothing she could do for him. No one else and nothing else came down that wagon track. But Andy still stood guard watching for more blue smoke and not knowing why.

Andy saw movement between the trees. Andy gripped the revolver handle tighter in his hand. It turned out to be mostly blue uniforms moving toward them along the wagon track. They were too far away to make out who they were, but he figured they should be Union soldiers and not rebels. Andy relaxed his grip on the revolver when he made out the shape of Digger marching back with a small band of recruits from his battle with the rebel menace a short time ago.

In the lead, there were three ragtag bearded prisoners followed by three bayonet-carrying recruits in blue. The rest of the soldiers held their muskets at the ready for use.

Andy was not sure how many went on the mission, but at this distance, he could see that not all of them were returning. He felt sickened at the thought of losing Twitch or any the others.

"They're not all returning … where are the rest?" Andy mumbled half aloud, "Just more funerals to attend."

Saddened, he lowered his weapon. It felt too heavy to hold up in his hand any longer. Andy looked down at the dead bearded man. He was lying face down in the dirt, crumpled up like a rag doll tossed on the side of the wagon tracks.

Isaac removed the dead man's weapons and went through his pockets. "Nothing in the pockets Andy."

Next, Isaac took the rebel's weapons and ammunition to the wagon. Andy took a good look at the dead man. Andy could not see an exit wound in the back of the head, but the rebel spy lay dead. Andy started to doubt if his lead slug killed the rebel. He silently questioned himself. Did I just take a man's life? Was it the lead slug from this revolver? Or am I fooling myself that I killed him?

He bent down and rolled the man over. He saw there was a bloody bullet hole in his bearded cheek. Andy heard someone calling to them, he looked up and saw Digger stop and wave at them to bring up the wagons.

They did not leave the rebel corpses where they fell. Instead, Sanders ordered some recruits to help Isaac load the four bodies onto the lead wagon.

In the lead wagon, Isaac and Jacob stopped by Digger, who took a good look at the dead rebel spies, "It looks like you got a couple of them. Who shot all of them? Wait a minute!"

Digger stared at the corpses, he stopped speaking and pointed at the bearded man that Andy shot. Digger excitedly said, "Yep, that's the one alright. I thought he escaped. He's the one who ordered the others to bury me alive, and this one and that one over there held me down. I'll never forget their faces."

Andy looked at Digger and nervously forced a small smile. He nodded his head as he sighed, thinking the others were dead and gone, "How many did we lose?"

Smiling, Digger was more relaxed now and teased Andy, "Why, you should know better. We didn't lose anyone, though a few of us got hit with some pretty big tree splinters when the rebel sharpshooters fired off only one round of return fire. Fortunately, we were right about the saplings messing up their aim, and they only splintered some trees rather than hitting us."

Chuckling some more, Digger told them. "We even got more prisoners than I expected, but I'm satisfied we pulled this mission off successfully. Now get our wagons up there to join Twitch and the rest."

Isaac asked, "How many rebels did you boys kill?"

Digger lowered his voice and quietly replied, "Three dead rebels, two wounded and all the living can still walk. There are nine prisoners in total. The captain will be pleased with all the questioning he'll be able to do."

Twitch ordered his men to lay the rebel bodies next to the wagon track for easier loading onto the wagons. He kept the remaining prisoners under a tight watch because no one was allowed to speak to the prisoners, especially since all the prisoners refused to talk.

While waiting for Jacob and the wagons to arrive, Twitch sent out a couple of scouts to find the rebels' base camp, as it had to be somewhere nearby.

Twitch's scouting party returned. However, rather than hiking back on foot, they rode in on handsome steeds. Each scout towed a string of horses, all of which were saddled up. Along with the horses were six fully loaded pack mules with food, camping and cooking gear. "Twitch, we found these horses and mules tethered by a spring at the base of the hill."

Twitch grinned from ear to ear as he stroked the mane of the lead stallion. "Now this is what I call a mount! He's not your common Union Army nag. Just look at him! He's unmistakably a cavalry horse raised to run like the wind, and I bet he's a real fighter too. Oh, what beautiful eyes you have."

He gave the horse a fatherly hug. It was as if Twitch was welcoming home his prodigal son. The horse responded and nuzzled his shoulder as if asking for forgiveness.

Digger walked in on this, "Twitch, don't get all maudlin over that fleabag horse. Why you just might make us all cry at finding your long-lost son!"

Twitch jokingly replied, "I wonder who his mother is?" He and everyone else broke out into a good laugh.

Twitch asked his scouts, "No signs of a camp anywhere nearby?"

"Nothing within a mile, sir, except for a hermit's hut west of here, but no one was there."

"A hermit?" questioned Twitch.

A scout replied, "That's right, sir. All the kids know him, we think of him as the spirit of the woods. He's lived out here for a couple of years and is harmless."

Twitch stood there watching most of the recruits shake their heads in agreement. "Alright, I guess some people are best left alone. Now, I can't have my privates wasting shoe leather when there are such fine mounts available. Come on lads, take a horse until we finish this expedition and get back to camp."

They tied the mule strings to the back of the tailgates and laid the bodies carefully and respectfully on the wagon with the other corpse.

Digger teased Jacob, "Is this hiding place much further? Or do we have to go all the way to Boston to find those crates?" Everyone burst out laughing.

Jacob did not reply because his ears were still ringing from Andy shooting over his shoulder, so he just smiled and nodded his head in agreement.

The expedition was just pulling out of sight when Falsemouth painfully awoke in the woods. He limped after them with one thought on his hateful mind, "Revenge."

CAVES OF MISERY

Jacob laughed, "We're almost there. It's just around the bend. At the base of the hill is the old quarry. That's where I hid the crates in the old Misery Hill Copper Mine at the far end of the quarry."

Sure enough, the quarry was about a quarter mile past the stone wall. The expedition arrived without further incident. Twitch looked around from atop his horse and said, "Jacob, I don't see any crates here, where are they?"

Jacob climbed off the wagon and headed behind a slagheap. He was glad the ringing in his ears finally stopped and his hearing had returned, "Over here gentlemen."

They followed him around the slagheap, and they discovered the entrance to an old boarded up mine. On the top beam hung the remains of a broken sign with just one legible word on it, "Misery."

As Andy, Digger, Jacob, and Twitch headed for the mine, Andy asked, "Why did you hide the crates in the old copper mine?"

Jacob grinned, "Andy, I thought you knew the story?"

Looking a bit skeptical Andy responded, "I've heard weird tales about this place, but never been out here before. What happened out here?"

Jacob was pleased he had an audience wanting to hear his tale, "Well, it's the kind of place nobody wants to be around because it's supposed to be haunted."

He laughed and continued his tale, "Andy as you know, none of the locals will come near the quarry or mine because of the murderous tales about strange haunting noises and spooky lights seen in and around here."

Jacob paused at the mine entrance to check the boards he nailed across the tunnel entrance, "Good, no one has been here. Twitch, I'll need a few men to pull off these boards, and we'll be out of here in no time at all. Then when we finish, we should nail them back on again. No sense in risking the lives of some stupid kid or dumb animal getting hurt in there after we leave."

With a bit of effort, Twitch and Andy began pulling the boards off the mine entrance. Jacob briefly stepped away.

Digger was a bit unsure about this whole haunted mine idea, "Jacob, how did it get haunted anyway?"

Jacob grinned at the chance to tell his ghost story to them, "Back in 1689 just like in Salem, the Mercyville townsfolk had witch problems, and they resolved the situation by executing the witches on top of this hill owned by Markus Malcolm Misery right above this sandstone quarry."

He pointed to the top of the quarry, "One day the townsfolk were hanging a witch right up there. Sorry, but I forget her name. Anyway, their newly erected makeshift scaffolding collapsed into the hill, and the townsfolk climbed down into the sinkhole to make sure she was dead. They discovered the main cavern but could not find her. She had vanished."

He paused for dramatic effect, "However, the executioner Markus Malcolm Misery tripped over a forty-two-pound copper nodule sticking out of the cavern floor near the broken scaffolding, and this started the great Misery Hill Copper Rush."

Then Jacob remembered the creepy story teaser he always added to the end of the tale, "Oops, I almost forgot the best part. Back then the townsfolk thought the witch had turned herself into the copper nodule. Markus Misery dug her up and melted her down into a large copper ingot. Mysteriously, it had her image on it. He put it on display in his barn, and charged people a halfpenny to see it."

Jacob continued, "The townsfolk thought the ingot was cursed so in 1754 when the French and Indian War started, he melted down the ingot for gunmetal and cast a small cannon."

Digger was confused, "Jacob, if the copper ingot was bad luck. Why would a cannon be good luck?"

Jacob laughingly replied, "The townsfolk figured anything fired from the cannon would be bad luck for those standing in front of it. They were right too. It played a pivotal role in the Battle of Montreal to help end the war.

"After the war, it was returned to Mercyville. Then when the Revolutionary War started, it was used by the Continental Army to fight the British, and according to legend it never missed. You can see it in the Mayor's front yard across from the old town hall."

Digger's eyes got big, and talking fast said, "Jacob, you tell a good yarn. So, they tried to hang her and found copper instead and forged a cannon out of her to fight the French and then the British. Huh! I've heard lots of yarns, but this is a pretty good yarn."

Jacob moved the story along, "That's right Digger. But nowadays these hills are full of abandoned and played out copper mines and sinkholes. Every once in a while, some poor animal falls into one of the sinkholes, for a sad death."

Jacob caught his breath, "Think of this place as the last remains of the first great gold rush in New England only with copper instead. It's said the mines go on for miles and miles underground starting here. Some legends claim the tunnels go all the way back to Mercyville. While other legends claim as far as Bolton Notch, but no one can prove it. My great grandfather mapped most of the tunnel system in his diary, and I have never stepped into the mine without it."

Digger nervously asked, "Do you mean to say the tunnels are haunted by executed witches and miners killed by cave-ins and animals that fell into the sinkholes?"

"Nah, it was mostly British prisoners of war who died in there during the Revolutionary War. The copper mine was played out by the early 1770s when Markus Misery went bankrupt, and the land was auctioned off and bought up by Isaiah Katz. With the start of the Revolutionary War, a new opportunity came along for Katz. He rented the mine out as a prison to hold the British officers captured by George Washington."

He continued his story, "The caverns were a natural prison for the thirty to forty British officers chained to the cave walls at any one time. It was cold and damp, and many of them fell ill and died of consumption. The locals say you can still hear them coughing and hacking in the cold recesses of the mineshafts. I believe one British officer was shot in the quarry while trying to escape."

Andy hollered, "Ok! We got the entrance cleared."

Jacob replied, "Hold on. I dragged the crates through the tunnel into the main cavern. We need some lanterns."

After being buried alive in the cemetery and hearing the witch tale, Digger would not go anywhere near the old mine. Cautiously he spoke up, "Twitch, why don't you check out the mine first, to make sure it's safe and the crates are still in there? I'll keep an eye on the wagons … and the prisoners."

On the other hand, Twitch could not wait to get in there to explore, "Digger, you're right there's no sense in causing any uncalled-for danger to the men. I'll take a scouting party into the mine. Come on. Let's take four lanterns each to set up in the tunnel and the cavern where Jacob hid the crates."

Once inside the mine, Jacob spoke softly, "Please, no loud noises and whatever you do, do not bump the soft sandstone walls or they will crumble and might collapse on us. As for the roof supports, they are all old and rotten. I don't want to be buried alive in here." Holding his lit lantern high, he led them.

Andy was getting nervous in the narrow tunnel, "I sure hope it ain't much further. I feel as though these walls are closing in on me."

Jacob quietly tried to reassure Andy, "Not to worry. All of us should be getting that closed-in feeling because the copper miners dug out the main tunnel walls angling inward. The tunnel passageway narrows a foot and a half as we go deeper into the mine. The narrowest part of the tunnel is right at the sharp corner into the entrance of the main cavern. It's up ahead. Remember when we go to leave, please be very careful not to bump the sides of the sharp corner as we carry the crates out."

They passed a small cavern, and Twitch looked into it. Cobwebs were covering an old mining cart broken down just inside the entranceway. He whispered to Jacob, "I take it the crates are in the main cavern? I hate spiders and crawly things. Is it much further?"

Jacob replied, "Ah, it's not that far to the main cavern. Just a few more steps past this sharp corner and we are home free. See, thank goodness, we can all breathe easier now, we're there."

Jacob vanished around the corner, and the rest followed.

The tunnel widened into an illuminated giant red-walled cavern. After the darkness of the tunnel, everyone was surprised at how bright it was in the main cavern. From above, there were shafts of bright sunlight streaming down onto the cavern floor.

Andy loudly exclaimed, "Wow! Never in a million years, would I believe this cavern was here!"

A fine mist of reddish sandstone dust rained down on them. Andy nervously looked at the others. Everyone went silent looking up at the grand cavern's ceiling. They all wondered the same thing - was it going to collapse?

Jacob whispered in hushed tones, "Don't worry Andy, I don't step nowhere down here without my great grandfather's diary because every page has maps and descriptions of the Misery Copper Mine tunnel system."

Andy and Twitch stood in awe at the height of the ceiling and grand size of the cavern. Andy commented, "You could easily fit the Mercyville Train Station down here with plenty of room to spare for a steam engine or two. Where's the light coming from?"

They craned their necks upwards to look for the light source in the cathedral-like ceiling. Twitch who was awestruck pondered, "I wonder if this is what it feels like to be in the Roman Pantheon. I read about that place once in a library and even saw a drawing of it in a book."

Jacob nervously laughed, "You're looking up at the witch's sinkhole and half a dozen or so air shaft openings the miners dug out through the hilltop. They dug those holes in the ceiling for air circulation and to let the sunlight in during the day, and this is one tunnel system with plenty of air in it. If the entrance tunnel ever collapsed, you would not suffocate. But there's no way to climb out, so you might starve or freeze to death before anyone ever found you." He nervously laughed, but no one else did, as a little more reddish sandstone dust sprinkled down on top of them.

Jacob pointed across the cavern and quietly said, "The crates are under that canvas tarp. I stacked them away from the witch's sinkhole and the air shaft in the cavern roof over here and covered the crates."

Twitch asked Jacob, "What do you want us to do with the lanterns?"

"Ah, turn the lanterns off and leave them on the floor next to the crates, so we don't forget them."

Twitch turned to Jacob, "Coming in through the tunnel, I noticed we only needed a couple of lanterns in a few places between the entrance and here. Is there any place we can hang some lanterns along the tunnel so we will be hands-free to carry out the crates?"

Jacob thought for a moment, "Good idea! I know where the old hangers are in the tunnel. I'll hang my four and be right back. Do you want me to bring in the first pair of soldiers? I can bring them in through the tunnel."

Jacob took his four lanterns and rushed into the tunnel before Andy and Twitch could say anything.

Twitch and Andy quickly uncovered the crates and arranged them in rows of four, making it easier to pick up the heavy cases. Twitch counted them, "Twelve crates … that must have been a heavy load for Jacob to haul in here."

Jacob finished lighting the tunnel and was back just in time to hear Twitch's comment. Sheepishly he responded, "They're heavy as you can see from the drag marks. I had a tough time dragging them in here. I made two wagon trips with no one to help me. I didn't open any of the crates, for all I know, the crates could be filled with rocks."

Twitch thought for a moment, "You didn't open any of them, huh. That would have been the first thing I would have done!"

"Twitch, you can open them outside for all I care. I just want to get out of here." Jacob continued, "I was afraid of being discovered. Can we just get them out of here? This place gets to me after a while. My great-grandfather, and later my grandfather, were killed by cave-ins in this Misery Copper Mine, not far from this spot."

Twitch tended to agree with Jacob about the copper mine. It was starting to bother him too. "Okay, let's get a move on here. Jacob, lead the first two men in here to get one crate out and remind them how crumbly the walls are. Then bring in more men to carry the rest of the crates out."

Andy and Twitch watched as Jacob started back up the tunnel. Twitch figured with two men carrying each crate they would have a much easier time than Jacob had when he dragged each container into the cavern by himself.

Andy and Twitch waited for Jacob to lead the first recruits there. It seemed to take forever for Jacob to bring them through. Getting impatient he said, "Andy let's get going. Grab that first crate with me, and we will lug it over to the entrance and save some time for the men carrying it out."

Together Andy and Twitch lifted up the first crate and started carrying it out of the cavern. As they neared the main tunnel, they heard a scream echo from the entrance, "Get back! Get back! Run!"

Andy swore it sounded like Angela screaming. They heard sounds of someone running towards them from the tunnel entrance. It was cut off by a ground-shaking explosion from far off that nearly knocked them off their feet. Momentarily stunned, they regained their balances as they could hear the entranceway collapsing in a rolling thunder of sandstone.

Twitch hollered, "Quick! Run for your life!"

Both men dropped the crate and started running across the cavern, trying to get as far away from the cave in as possible. They were about two dozen yards away when the wall behind them started to collapse in thick clouds. Twitch hollered, "Cover your nose and mouth with your bandana!"

Reddish-brown dust roiled up across the open cavern, engulfing the two running men in a massive dust storm. They kept running with their bandanas pressed tightly against their noses and mouths.

CHAPTER ELEVEN

The reddish sandstone dust still choked them through their bandanas and blinded their exposed eyes. They made it across the cavern and huddled together on the far side of the main cavern away from the cave-in. All they could do was bury their bandana-covered faces in their coat sleeves and wait it out until the dust settled before they dared to try getting out.

Every once in a while, Twitch or Andy would peek out just enough to try to get a glimpse of the cavern, but every time the dust would sting their eyes. So, they would pull their heads back into their thick woolen jackets like snapping turtles just below the surface of a pond.

As time rolled on, Andy's ears were still ringing from the thunder of the cave-in, and he had trouble hearing anything at all. Twitch yelled something to Andy and then poked him in the ribs when he did not respond. "Take a look! I can see the far wall through the dust. It looks like the cave-in was a total collapse. Let's see if we can find a way out of here. I don't want to set up housekeeping down here. Leave your bandana on as the air still hasn't completely cleared."

Andy could barely see Twitch get up, much less hear anything he said. Andy stood up and looked around, and saw Twitch pointing back from where they had just come. He watched Twitch head back to the collapsed entrance. Andy followed him, trying to walk on top of the unstable rubble. The two of them made their way back to the cavern tunnel entrance, only to find it wholly blocked by the avalanche of red sandstone.

Just as Andy was about to yell for help, Twitch stopped him, "Andy if you yell or fire a shot or two, it will bring the roof down on us. Besides, unless someone is standing on the edge of one of the air shafts, no one is going to hear either of us."

Concerned Andy asked, "Twitch, do you think the men Jacob was leading in all got out in time?"

Twitch shook his head, "I hope so, but from the sound of Jacob's scream that we heard, I think we may have lost a man or two, including Jacob I'm afraid. If the outside wall in the quarry crumbled and gave way, we may be the only survivors."

Andy's felt sickened over the loss of any of their men, "What do you think the explosion was?"

"Andy, I've heard a lot of black powder explosions in my life, but this time it sure sounded like Alfred Nobel's invention to end all wars, dynamite. At least three sticks would be about right to bring the entrance way down on our heads."

Andy ruminated on that for a moment, and he remembered their crate, "Hey Twitch, do you see our first crate anywhere in this slag heap of red rocks and sand?"

Twitch looked around, "I think we were about ten more feet closer to the entrance when it collapsed. If I am right, it looks like the rocks would have pushed the crate over this way. Let's try over there. Come with me."

They made their way carefully across the debris field looking for any sign of the crate.

The ground was uneven, and the rocks and stones were wobbly, "Andy, believe it or not, I think I found it. Get over here and help me dig it out."

Sure enough, Andy spotted the edge of a corner sticking out of the rubble. They quickly shifted the debris out of the way and started to drag the crate to the other side of the cavern. That's when Andy spotted the mangled hand poking out of the rubble, "Twitch, someone didn't make it, look over there."

Twitch let go of the crate and headed over to the hand, "Come here Andy! It's only right to dig him out and identify who he is and give him a proper burial. After all, that could have been one of us under there."

To their shock, it was Jacob. Andy started to shake and tear up. Twitch sadly said, "Come on Andy! We don't have time for nerves. Give me a hand over here. We have to finish the job and give him a proper burial."

Together the two of them dug Jacob out. Twitch picked up Jacob and carried him away from the rubble. He laid Jacob down near the lanterns on the other side of the cavern. "Help me go through his pockets. He may have something like a pocket knife or matches or something else that will help us get out of here alive."

That is when Andy remembered what Jacob told him about his great grandfather's diary, and how he never stepped anywhere inside the cave system without it, "Twitch, look for a book in his pockets."

Andy turned away, unable to watch Twitch go through Jacob's pockets and search the clothes of his friend's crumpled body.

Twitch grumbled, "How's a book going to help us out of here?" He still searched Jacob's clothes for it, as he finished the grim task, Twitch said, "Andy, there is nothing in his pockets. Not even a scrap of paper to start a fire with."

"Twitch, it has to be in one of his pockets. He said he never stepped anywhere down here without his great grandfather's diary so look again."

Twitch knowingly grinned, and started to squeeze the boots, "Andy, you're sure he said he never stepped anywhere without the diary, right?"

"That's what he said. Twitch, it has to be in his pockets somewhere. Jacob said that he never stepped anywhere ..."

That is when it dawned on Andy what Jacob meant, "Wait a minute Twitch. Look in his boots."

Andy looked down, and Twitch was holding up the diary, sighing Twitch said, "I found it stuffed on the inside of his left boot. Here, hold onto it for me, while I lift him up."

Andy felt funny taking the diary. He started to tear up, but he knew it might save them. As Twitch lifted up Jacob, Andy half mumbled to himself, "Thank you, Jacob, for your great grandfather's diary. I'm sure the maps are in good condition and using his diary we will find a way out of these caves of misery. Amen."

Twitch picked a nearby spot, "Let's get Jacob buried, and one of the crates opened. I'm dying to find out what's so important in it."

Andy watched as Twitch removed Jacob's coat before burying him. "We may need it later for splints or something else so trust me."

At first, Andy thought it disgusting to take a dead man's coat, but if it helped them to survive, then it was still useful to the living. Just as a diary, it is useful for survival, or was it? He stopped thinking about it and helped Twitch cover the body with more rocks and stones.

They laid Jacob to rest in the far corner of the cavern and covered his body with lots of loose rocks and stones. They even found a three-foot piece of broken mine board to use for the tombstone. Andy carved Jacob's name and today's date on it with his pocketknife.

Twitch, being the oldest, and in charge, gave the last rights by saying the Lord's Prayer and a few kind words about Jacob.

Andy got a bit teary eyed some more. Trying to console Andy, Twitch said, "Come on Andy. Jacob would not have told you about the diary if he didn't want us to get out of here." Still choked up a bit, Andy nodded his head yes.

They headed back to the crate and dragged it out of the rubble and over to the side of the cavern. Both men collapsed, exhausted. Andy mumbled, "I didn't think it was that much effort to dig it out, but it must have been." Both were breathing heavy now.

"Andy, we were almost killed, and we buried our friend and dragged out this dead weight of a crate. We're still breathing in way too much dust. We have to get out of here until the dust settles. We'll head up this side tunnel over there and rest up for a while."

Andy checked his watch, it was just past three in the afternoon, "Twitch, it's three-twelve. With how hungry I feel, I swore it was later in the day than that."

"Same here Andy. I wish we had grabbed some hardtack from the wagon before we came in, but we didn't. While we rest, let's check the remaining eight lanterns and consolidate the fuel in them. By right, six of the lanterns should still be full and only a little bit of oil used. We only lit two lanterns when we first came through the tunnel. These lanterns burn a long time. Altogether, I figure after we distribute the whale oil between them, we should have more than enough oil if we're stuck here overnight and for our trek out of here."

They both grinned ear to ear and started to check the whale oil. The first lantern was almost empty and the second one was not even half full. Andy realized they would not have enough whale oil for more than a couple of the lanterns, "Twitch, didn't Birdy say someone filled all the lanterns this morning?"

"Come to think of it. You're right Andy. Why do you ask?"

"I just poured the oil from two lanterns into one, and it's not half full. I smell a rat back at camp."

"Let's not worry about it just yet. We can only fill what we have."

With less fuel per lantern, they finished redistributing the whale oil in a matter of minutes. "Andy, how many working lanterns do we have?"

"Three full lanterns and the fourth is maybe a quarter full." Andy sighed, "I don't get it because we couldn't have burned that much fuel. Could we have somehow spilled it out along the wagon tracks?"

Twitch sighed, "No Andy. Someone back at camp lied to Birdy and didn't fill the lanterns. We will not know for sure who it is until we get back. Now we will have to wait until sunrise before we can search for a way out. If we use all of them, we will not be able to find our way around down here for some time. I do not want to die down here, do you? Come on! Let's get out of this dust. Grab one end of the crate."

Together they half-dragged and carried the crate up the dark tunnel, and soon reached another cavern, but it was much smaller. The sunlight and air were still plentiful, so they took off their bandanas as they sat down to rest for a while.

They both slept fitfully on the hard cavern floor, only waking up to a slight chill in the air as the sunlight began to fade. Twitch saw Andy check his father's watch.

With no lanterns and still tired and sore from burying Jacob and digging out the crate, they both decided to call it a night.

"Hey Twitch?" Andy quizzed him.

"What is it, Andy?"

"What do you think is in our crate that the mayor wants to keep secret?"

Twitch got up, looked around and picked up a choice heavy rock to use as a hammer. He started to hit one of the corner slats of wood on the side of the crate.

ESCAPE FROM CHAOS

Andy watched Twitch trying to get the lid off the crate, for what seemed like forever. Finally, the sideboard started pulling away from the crate. It came loose enough for Twitch to get his long fingers into the opening to try prying it off by hand. By prying the lid upwards, he eventually got it to pull away from the crate with just enough room for him to slide his bare hands under the lid. Bracing himself, he pulled up hard on the slats until he finally had the crate open.

They both looked into the crate and saw layers of oiled brown packing paper. The kind of paper used to wrap cast iron bars to keep them from rusting and brass bars from tarnishing, Twitch grinned when he saw the oil paper, "Good this paper will make great fire starters, maybe even short-lasting torches in a pinch."

Lifting the top layer of paper, Twitch found and removed a watertight waxed package. Handing it off to Andy, he looked back into the crate. Removing more oilpaper, he exposed the tops of some wrapped solid cylinders standing on end.

Twitch gently reached inside and paused. He looked into his friend's eyes, and cleared his dry throat, "Andy you may want to leave this cavern just in case it explodes. It might be some new munitions or explosives, so you may want to get out of range in case it goes off."

Andy looked around the cavern, "Ah Twitch, there ain't no place to go that won't collapse. Besides I would rather die fast than starve to death slowly down here. Do whatever you have to do. Let's get this over with."

Taking a deep breath Twitch blessed himself and reached in, he gently dug his short fingernails between the oilpaper wrappers. Seizing one of the cylinders, he gently lifted it upwards. Nervous and sweating profusely, he slowly extracted it out of the crate. He now held what looked like a wrapped cylinder in the palm of his hand, "Andy this is way too heavy to be any explosives I've ever handled before. It must be something new and deadly."

As he tried to open the oily paper wrapper, the cylinder slipped out of his hands. As it fell, they both cringed waiting for an explosion. Instead, it hit the floor with a loud clunk noise. An oiled paper tube broke open spilling gold coins between their feet.

Chapter Twelve

Relieved that they were not dead, they both stared at the shiny contents. Twitch bent down and picked up a handful of coins. He handed some to Andy to examine.

"Andy who would ever believe these crates contained a golden hoard." Twitch stopped in midsentence when he saw Mayor Katz's face embossed on the gold coin in his hand.

Andy and Twitch held up one coin after another examining each in the fading daylight. Mayor Katz's face was stamped on to the front of every piece of gold.

On closer examination, they both started laughing as they read the inscription below the mayor's image, "In Katz We Trust 1861."

As Andy and Twitch held up one coin after another examining the same profile on all of the gold pieces, they continued laughing, that is until they turned the coins over. Their smiles quickly faded and turned to shocked disgust. On the back of every coin was a small cherub and beneath it was the inscription:

"Republic of Katz the Twelfth Confederate State of America in Katz We Trust"

Andy disgustedly dropped his handful of coins back into the crate. He tried to wipe his hands clean of the whale oil on his pants.

Twitch thought about the gold coins he picked up, "Andy we can't let these get back into Katz's hands. In the morning we need to hide this crate before we move out. We both need to pocket a few of them to show the captain. These little golden confederate dollars give us the evidence the Union needs to convict and hang the traitorous Mayor Katz and his conspirators."

The light continued to fade as Andy opened his Dad's pocket watch, "It's almost seven o'clock, I think today's sunset is in about a half hour. Twitch where do you want to try to sleep tonight?"

Twitch looked around the cavern for a place to spend the night. There was nowhere else to bed down for the night except on the cavern floor. "Andy, I hate sleeping on the ground. What about you?"

Chapter Twelve

Andy did not look forward to sleeping on the rock floor, "I'm all in favor of moving on, but we don't know anything about the tunnel system to quickly move through it. I flipped through the diary, and it is full of warnings about dead drops and pits as well as crumbling air shafts and dry wells."

Hoping for a quick way out Twitch asked, "I take it there are no exits nearby, Andy?"

"I can look, but we would have to use up the whale oil tonight. I think we should try to save it for our escape out of these tunnels."

Twitch thought about it, "Back in the main cave I seem to remember seeing at the far end of it a pile of old creosote soaked wooden tunnel supports. Maybe we can get a fire going out there, at least we will be warm for tonight."

Andy nodded in agreement, "What do you want me to do with this package we found?"

Twitch snapped back, "Right now we need to focus on getting out of here. Stuff it in your boot." Andy did and quickly forgot about it. They hurriedly gathered up the rest of the dropped gold coins, and then gathered together the lanterns.

Leaving the gold coin-filled crate behind, they hiked back toward the main cavern, and made it back before the last of the sunlight vanished.

Twitch and Andy headed straight for the wood pile. They picked through the dry rotted pieces and picked up a good armload of halfway decent broken pieces of lumber for a campfire. They needed some kindling to get the fire started for the upcoming cold night.

Twitch went over to the empty whale oil lanterns picked up a few and brought them over. "Andy the wicks should still have enough oil soaked up in them for us to easily ignite wood." Regretfully he added, "I should have brought back the oil paper, but forgot it."

He and Andy cranked out a couple of wicks placing them strategically under the wood. "Andy, do you have any kitchen matches on you?"

"You know what Twitch, I do have some matches."

Chuckling Andy pulled off a boot and shook it upside down a small tin dropped out. He handed it to Twitch. "I grabbed this small tin of matches when I went to the Tobacconist to get Mayor Katz's Cuban cigar order the other day. I forgot I still had them in my pocket when I joined up and stuck the tin in my shoe. Then when I got my uniform, I stuffed it in the toe of my boot."

Twitch chuckled while looking at the matches, "Thank Goodness for modern conveniences. I remember my grandfather telling me how he gave a grocer a day's pay for a tin box of matches just like this one."

The first match easily lit the oil-soaked wicks, and a warm fire soon spread through the creosote covered pine timbers. The warmth felt good to both of them. Andy used the firelight to flip through and read the diary. He paid careful attention to the hand-drawn maps and tunnel route agendas in the book. Twitch kept the fire burning to give off enough light for Andy to read late into the night. Andy eventually fell asleep while examining a map in the diary.

Twitch holding a handful of the gold coins wondered why certain things happened. Who told Matthews that Nick would be at the station? Who was tipped off again about Nick being at the old town hall? Moreover, who tipped off the rebel spies about Jacob and the route he was taking to the mine when even he did not know where they were going? Who tricked Digger into going to the cemetery so he could be killed? And who failed to fill the oil lamps?

However, the questions that nagged him the most was who threw the sticks of dynamite into the tunnel? And where did he get it? He also worried about Digger and the rest. Were they killed in the avalanche following the mine entrance cave in? Twitch finally fell asleep with more questions than answers.

It was almost pitch black in the cavern when Andy and Twitch woke up, "Andy what time is it?" Twitch inquired.

"I don't know it's too dark to see the time. Do we have any wood left for the fire?" Before Andy could say anything else, he saw embers starting to glow as if someone was trying to reignite the fire, "I sure hope that's you and not some ghost blowing on those embers."

He heard Twitch laugh, "Of course it's me, I ain't no ghost yet. However, if you give me a couple of days down here with no water I will gladly haunt you."

A piece of whale oil-soaked wick flamed up under some kindling, and the glow of embers turned into a weak campfire light. "Andy, I would not wait too long to see what time it is because the flame is already starting to die out."

Andy shivered in the cold, and said, "Five Thirty-five. It's downright freezing in here. Do we have any more pieces of timber we can throw on the fire?"

In the flickering light, Andy could barely make out Twitch carefully piling some pieces on the small fire. In a matter of minutes, the creosote-soaked wood flamed up enough to take the chill out of their bones.

"Twitch, when do you think we should start looking for a way out?"

Twitch thought about it awhile before answering, "I think we have the best chance of getting out if we wait until sunrise. That way we at least have the light coming in through the air shafts to help guide us once in a while. We might even be able to climb out of one of the larger air shafts."

Andy was silent for a minute or two before he agreed, "Sunrise should be about six-thirty-seven this morning. I can wait about an hour or so."

"Andy, what did you do, eat an almanac when you were a kid?"

Chuckling Andy replied, "No, someone added a sunrise and sunset table to the back of the diary. Do you want to borrow it?"

Twitch teased Andy, "We're almost out of timber for the fire. If it starts to go out, can I use the diary pages as kindling?"

Andy replied with a resounding echo, "No!"

Soon they both dozed off again. The cold dawn light woke them, even though it was too early for any sunbeams to warm the cavern up.

They stuffed their pockets with small pieces of kindling to make a fire later. Twitch removed all the remaining whale oil-soaked wicks and stuffed them into one of the empty lantern bases for easy carrying.

Andy found a pickaxe with a splintered handle. At first, he thought it might somehow come in handy, but he already had too much to carry along with him.

Together they were an unsightly pair covered in reddish dust and dirt, lugging their lanterns and other things as they searched for a way out of the complex tunnel system. They got to the side-tunnel entrance leading to other caverns and down into the lower levels of the mine. They lit a lantern.

Andy stopped at the entrance to show Twitch the diary's first map page, "Twitch, here is one of the map pages. It shows the side tunnels and dugout galleries. Over here is the main cavern we just left, and over there is the cavern where we left the crate of rebel gold. This map shows three pitfalls and an underground gorge and even a waterfall with a note about safe potable water. I think we should head there first."

Twitch did not hesitate to answer him, "You're right we will have a better chance of getting out if we can get some water in us - that way we will keep our strength longer."

Twitch added, "To me that hand-drawn map and scribblings make no sense at all. The diary is chaos to me. Andy, I leave the diary in your hands to decide our best route out of here. Lead the way out Private."

Andy nodded his head and said, "Alright, let's go hide the gold crate and find some water. I sure wish Birdy had given us some canteens instead of only a water barrel on one of the wagons."

They walked the short distance to the gold crate and found it untouched right where they had left it, and looked around but did not find a hiding place for it. So, they moved it to a far corner to keep it out of direct sight from the main tunnel entrance to that cavern. Both of them slipped some of the coins into their pockets to give to the captain.

Heading down the main tunnel, they started their search for the branch to the waterfall. Twitch asked, "How big do you think the waterfall is? Do you think maybe the size of Niagara Falls? That would be something to see underground, wouldn't it?"

Andy chuckled, "If so, we'd be flushed out into the quarry and riding the rapids down into Lake Katz."

They both laughed and were in good spirits as they slowly made their way through the tunnel. Every hundred yards they passed an air shaft.

They examined some airshafts trying to figure out how the miners ever dug out such narrow holes all the way to the surface. Other air shafts looked like natural holes to the surface. At every air shaft Twitch kept saying the same thing, "Andy, I don't think an eight-year-old could crawl up one of these air shafts to freedom much less one of us. Let's try the next one."

It was difficult for them to figure out how far they had hiked through all the twists and turns of the poorly lit tunnel system. They tried to count their steps on the uneven tunnel floors. It felt as if they had hiked miles. Whenever they checked the diary map, it showed their advance was always far less then what they thought it should be. They finally came to the first right fork in the tunnel.

Andy stopped walking, "Twitch, hold the lantern for me, while I recheck the map in the diary."

Holding up the diary pages in the lamplight Andy turned the book this way and that way trying to read the map. He even flipped the pages back and forth between the previous and next map pages.

"Hmm, Twitch I don't know. I think it's too early for this tunnel to be the waterfall branch. The map does not show this branch. There is nothing in the diary about the tunnel forking before the waterfall. The map only shows a bunch of numbered and unnumbered side tunnels before the right-hand tunnel to the waterfall. My best guess is we take this branch. Hopefully, it's the right one."

Handing the lantern back to Andy, Twitch said, "Just in case the diary is wrong, let's watch our step and go nice and slow. I get a bad feeling about this unmarked right branch tunnel."

They gingerly entered the right branch, but after a short distance, Andy decided to turn back, and he said, "There is something wrong with this branch. According to the map, there should be an alcove about ten feet in on the left. I counted my paces, and we have come twenty paces with no alcove. We better go back."

As Andy started to turn back, he felt himself lose his balance. He started to fall when the tunnel floor gave way underfoot. Twitch grabbed Andy's arm and pulled him back from the collapsing floor. They both lost their balance and fell backward away from the newly formed sinkhole. The lantern light vanished along with the rocks and dust tumbling down the sides of the now gaping sinkhole in the tunnel floor.

Sitting on the floor in total darkness, both of them gasped for air while the dust settled. "Andy that was a close call. For a moment I thought we were going to meet our maker. Let's get out of this branch tunnel before the sinkhole opens any more and swallows us up. Can you relight your lantern?"

In the dark Andy sighed sounding disgusted, "No, it's gone. I dropped it when I slipped and lost my balance. It vanished into the sinkhole along with its light. We need to light another."

Andy heard Twitch get up and fumble around in the total darkness as he slowly felt his way back up the tunnel a few steps.

Still petrified that he might fall into the sinkhole, Andy did not try to get up. A moment later Twitch illuminated the tunnel in the dull glow of a spare lantern. It was just enough light to see the walls and floor near them and to find their way back out.

Neither of them said another word until they were back in the central tunnel. Andy sheepishly remarked, "Twitch, thank you for saving me back there. Not only did I almost lose my life, but worse I almost lost you the diary back there. You'd have been stuck down here for sure with little hope of escaping."

Twitch sighed, "Let's not ruminate on that. I think we need to be more careful how we use the diary. Obviously, not all the tunnels, branches and caves are in it. Something tells me the miners kept expanding the tunnel system long after the maps were drawn up in it by Jacob's grandfather."

Andy nodded his head in agreement. They had little choice in the matter, but to use the diary. As they continued their underground trek through the tunnels, they were just a bit less hopeful as to their survival.

With the lantern in one hand and the diary in the other hand, Andy stopped at every side tunnel and looked for the tunnel number on the map and if it should be on their left or right. He thought he located the waterfall tunnel a couple of times, but each one had no alcove near the mouth. By now, they were getting dry mouthed and parched from the tunnel dust.

Twitch hoarsely croaked out, "We better find the waterfall soon." Exhausted and dehydrated, Andy did not even nod his head this time, he just kept shuffling his feet one-step at a time.

It seemed like forever before they came to a promising manmade tunnel. Hope returned to Andy when he saw a sign for the right path to follow.

"Twitch! Look! Someone nailed up a sign to that ceiling beam, do you think we should trust it?"

Twitch examined the broken hanging board with a single word of hope burned clumsily into the wood grain, probably by a hot iron poker or bar:

WATERFALL

Without hesitating he hoarsely replied, "It looks real to me, Andy, I'm parched let's take it."

They breathed a little easier now that they felt they were on the right path again. As the two slowly headed down this tunnel, the lantern ran out of whale oil, and it quickly grew dark. Twitch reached to grab another lamp, but he changed his mind, "Andy, I see a faint light up ahead. Maybe it's the waterfall cavern."

Andy and Twitch headed for the dim light, even though they were exhausted and parched. Hope returned with every step they took. Stepping into another cavern, they breathed in the fresh air from the airshafts. In the distance, a small waterfall about an arm's length wide flowed out of bedrock into an underground stream.

Near the waterfall, someone had set up some barrels to sit on around a rough-hewn plank table. Andy and Twitch headed over to it first. They piled their lanterns and stuff onto it. At the waterfall, they stuck their heads in the cold fresh falling water and drank their fill.

Picking a spot illuminated by a sunbeam, Andy sat down cross-legged on the cavern's sandstone floor. He popped open his pocket watch and smiled at his mom's picture. It was half past noon, no wonder they were tired and thirsty. They had trekked through the tunnels for the last six hours without a break.

He knew they still had a long way to go to get out, but he was exhausted. He dozed off while sitting there and still holding the open pocket watch. He dreamed of being with his mom on a picnic.

Twitch poked Andy's back, and rudely awoke Andy from his dream, "Andy, time to get up. We have to get out of here. We both fell asleep, and we have to get moving again. I found something to eat, and we can drink our fill at the waterfall and be on our way."

Looking around the cavern, Twitch nervously complained, "This place is starting to unnerve me, I think it might be one of Mayor Katz's or the rebels' secret hideouts. At the other end of the cavern, I discovered a lean-to built of freshly cut pinewood and a stack of firewood. Inside the lean-to, I found kitchen matches and a couple of large biscuit tins, and an empty canteen."

Twitch stopped to catch his breath, and then he continued, "Andy, there were plenty of fresh biscuits in the tins. So, I naturally liberated a couple of handfuls of biscuits for both of us, and the canteen, too. After all, we need water for the journey."

CHAPTER TWELVE

As Twitch spoke, Andy checked the time and discovered he had slept almost an hour. He bit into one of the biscuits. He was so hungry, and it tasted as good as his Aunt Abby's biscuits. He muttered half aloud, "Man, someone sure bakes like Aunt Abby."

He ate two of the biscuits Twitch had handed him and stuffed the other two in his pockets for later. He drank his fill of the clear cold water straight out of the waterfall and filled the canteen. He reluctantly prepared to leave this tranquil cavern, not knowing what to expect further down the tunnel.

"Twitch according to this diary, we can save some time if we don't go back the way we came in from the main tunnel. Instead, the diary map shows a tunnel running parallel to the main tunnel out of here. It rejoins the main tunnel way up here. What do you think?"

Twitch looked at the map, "What are those tiny crosshatches there on the map?"

Andy looked carefully at the pencil scratches on the page, "I don't know, but according to the diary this way is a lot shorter than backtracking to the main tunnel."

"Alright, let's try the parallel tunnel, we can always come back and sleep here tonight if we have to. We will have to be careful if I'm right about the rebels using this cavern."

They gathered their stuff and left the waterfall behind. This tunnel looked too well maintained, which made Twitch worry even more about the rebels, and his worrying started to unnerve Andy.

However, this tunnel was narrow and not well lit. When they rounded a sharp corner in the passage, they had an even greater concern. The journey suddenly ended on an abrupt narrow ledge in another cavern. As Andy stepped out of the tunnel, he almost went over that sharp ledge. Twitch grabbed the back of Andy's coat just in time and pulled him back. Andy gasped, "Thanks, Twitch."

Right in front of them was a bottomless pit blocking their path. A short way along their narrow ledge, they could see a rickety rope bridge across the chasm. Twitch stuttering nervously whispered, "Andy that thing doesn't look too safe to me. Let's go back."

They now knew what the pencil scratch marks in the diary meant. Twitch took a good look into the bottomless pit, and started to freak out, "No Andy! We're going back! I ain't crossing that rickety rope bridge. We are going back."

Twitch closed his eyes. When he opened them, Andy was already on the rope bridge and started pulling on the ropes. Andy yelled, "Twitch the ropes may not look the best, but they sure feel strong enough. In the summer I've tied up a lot of rope to swing from trees over the Housatonic River and dived in using ropes far worse than these ropes. These are good ropes. Let's cross! I'm dying to try it! Come on over! It looks like fun!"

Before Twitch could object, Andy was on the rope bridge halfway across the chasm, "Hey Twitch, watch this!"

Andy took one of the mayor's gold coins out of his pocket and flipped it into the middle of the chasm. They both froze not making a sound, waiting to hear the gold coin clink. About twelve seconds later they heard a faint clunk a long way off. Amazed at how long it took to hit bottom, Andy exclaimed, "Wow! I thought it would never hit bottom! Come on Twitch follow me!"

Twitch turned ash white and closed his eyes. He hollered, "Andy! You come right back here! Right now! It is too dangerous, get back here!" When he opened his eyes, he saw Andy sitting on the other side of the chasm dangling his feet over the edge of the cliff and laughing at him.

"Private Anders!" Twitch angrily yelled, "You just wait until I get my hands on you! Why you, laughing hyena! No one makes a fool of me!" His voice echoed in the cavern.

For the moment, Twitch forgot his fear of heights and rushed the rope bridge. He was halfway across when he nervously started to twitch and stutter that he was going to die. He stopped, frozen in place, halfway across the wobbly rope bridge.

Andy gasped, as he thought Twitch was going to pass out and fall. Instead, Twitch swallowed hard and began to slowly inch his way across the last half of the wobbly rope bridge.

Breathing heavily, Twitch collapsed on the ground next to Andy. In about a minute, he started to laugh, and Andy joined in, "See Andy, I told you it was perfectly safe. We're alive and well, aren't we." They laughed even more.

Laughingly, Andy, asked, "Who said it was safe Twitch? I seem to remember goading you and daring you to cross that rope bridge. Ah, why did you stop halfway across?"

Twitch looked at Andy, "Honestly, it was weird, my feet knew something that I didn't know. I was trying to turn around and go back, but my feet wouldn't budge. Then I felt a rope strand pop and my feet would only go forward. So, I followed them."

He got up, and nervously said, "Alright Andy, you win, I admit it, you got me to cross that bridge when I came to it. Now let's get going before we change our minds. I am not going back."

The two of them happily left the chasm behind. Oddly, the tunnel had more sunlit airshafts every hundred feet or so, with plenty of fresh air coming into the mine. Andy blew out his lantern. He inspected a couple of air shafts for a way out, but the air shafts were way too narrow to climb out. So, they continued on their way hoping to find an exit tunnel.

"Andy, is there anything in that diary that tells us where these tunnels end?"

Andy stopped to rest under an airshaft of bright light, "Hmm, sort of, see this arrow pointing off the top of the page. Right under it is the word Mercyville and on this other page over here, this arrow points to Bolton Notch. We are coming up to this crossroad in the tunnel where we have to decide whether to turn left to Mercyville or turn right to Bolton Notch."

As Andy flipped through the diary pages, he ruminated, "Somewhat weird, huh? There must be ten miles of tunnels down here. Someone went to a lot of effort to dig all these tunnels, and it was not for copper either. I'll bet those rebel spies are behind this tunnel system."

Now it was Twitch's turn to ask the questions, "Andy, it must be the rebel spies. Who else would want to attack Mercyville? But why Bolton Notch?"

Andy continued to ponder trying to figure out the bigger picture, "Mercyville is the tobacco-wrapper capitol of New England and has thread mills along the Housatonic River, and if you blow the Lake Katz dam, you wipe out the thread mills and half of Mercyville."

Twitch thought about it for about a minute, "That sounds possible. But doesn't the Mayor want to turn Mercyville into the twelfth Confederate State? What good would it do him if he destroyed his mills and the town?

What about Bolton Notch? That's just a few miles east of here. Is there anything strategic out there?"

Andy's eyes grew wide, "Eureka! I have it! This idea would fit in perfectly with the mayor's plan to join the rebels."

Andy explained what he figured out, "In Connecticut, the valleys run north to south. The railroad pass through Bolton Notch must be the rebel spies' real target because a small avalanche closed it five or six years ago for six months."

Andy continued, "If the spies dynamited the top off the Notch the explosion would start a large avalanche and fill in the pass. It would stop all trains running to and from Eastern Connecticut and Rhode Island for twenty miles north and south of here."

He finished up by saying, "So, if Mercyville becomes the Republic of Katz, then Katz would control the access route through southern New England for twenty miles all around Bolton Notch. No supply or troop trains could get through to the Union forces in the South. Come on Twitch! We have to get out of here and warn the captain."

They started on their way through the tunnel again. Air shafts in this part of the passageway were spaced close together and illuminated by natural light. As a result, Andy and Twitch were able to pick up their pace and were soon rushing through the tunnels in the fading afternoon light.

One of them tripped up and bounced off a support timber and the tunnel ceiling partially collapsed. They just barely escaped this minor rock fall with their lives, but with serious injuries.

Andy had sliced his thigh open on a splintered timber. Twitch took a hit to the head from falling rocks and collapsed unconscious on the edge of the debris field.

That last rock fall knocked some sense into Andy. All he wanted now was to get out alive, but he was quickly losing blood. He was getting woozier and more light-headed by the minute.

He looked up, blurry eyed, just making out lamp light bouncing off the tunnel walls in the distance, and coming towards them fast. He was unarmed and fearing that the rebel spies finally tracked them down. He decided he would not die without taking some of them with him. However, he did not realize how badly his leg was bleeding, and he started to pass out.

Before passing out, the last thing Andy vaguely remembered seeing was this bright light hovering over him, and the face of his Aunt Abby looking down upon him. Woozily he imagined he heard his mother's voice scolding him, "Andy Anders! What on earth are you doing down here? You're supposed to be dead! You're coming home with me right now young man!"

RETURN OF THE DEAD

Aunt Abby worried as the men carried Andy and Twitch through the tunnel system. They carefully lifted the two injured men up through the trapdoor. Once they were in the Mercyville Republic newspaper office, Aunt Abby asked, "Will someone please light the ceiling lamps? Woody, tonight's carload must go through, but what are we to do with Andy and Twitch? We cannot do both!"

Carefully, staying in the shadows, the six men and six women helped lift the two bodies out of the tunnel onto Woody's news print layout tables. Woody whispered, "Thank you. There's a paste bucket on the counter. I was going to use it to post those front pages around town today. Quick! Someone paste those front pages over the entire front window. We don't want any passerby to discover what we are doing in here."

A couple of women quickly pasted up newsprint across the front windows. Woody looked at the ragtag group of people now jammed into his print shop, "Thank you for helping us rescue our friends. Please, I need all of you to go back down into the tunnel and wait by the trap door ladder. We need to sort this unexpected delay out, and I promise you, one of us will be right down to help all of you get out of here safely."

For one of the rare times in her life, Abby was all nervous and panicky, "Woody, we can't just leave our guests in the tunnels until we get back, it would not be right. Someone has to look after them. Andy is family and as for the other soldier. Well, he's ah Union, and I'm sure he would agree with what we are doing and cooperate."

Woody's young apprentice Charlie spoke up, "Excuse me, Woody, but you both forgot about me. I have helped Aunt Abby dozens of times with our guests, and I can take them through the tunnels and lead them over the top of Bolton Notch along the secret trail to the next stop at the Miller's Barn."

Woody thought about it for a moment, "Charlie that's a good idea. Please take good care of them for us tonight. Be extra careful because the mayor's men are everywhere these days still searching for our guests. You had better get going it'll be sunrise soon. Thank you and may God bless you with a safe journey tonight."

Charlie quickly climbed down through the floor's trapdoor and pulled it closed. Aunt Abby promptly spread printers' sawdust over the trapdoor to make it blend in with the rest of the floor planks.

Woody continued to clean Andy's leg wound with the only thing he had, which was the alcohol he used to clean his printing plates. Next, he started suturing Andy's leg wound.

Briefly looking up at her, Woody continued, "Abby, thank you for your help tonight. Let's be grateful we have Charlie to run the railroad tonight, and that the minor rockfall did not block the escape tunnel. Luckily, we heard Andy delusional and calling out for his mother in the side tunnel. As it is, Andy has lost a lot of blood, and his wound might still claim either his leg or worse yet his life."

Aunt Abby, lamented, "Woody, we need to get them back to the inn to recover. As it is, everyone at Camp Mercyville thinks they're both dead. I wish we could take them straight to the field hospital, but how would we ever explain finding them."

With a shimmer of hope in her eyes, "Woody I've got an idea, can we move both of them soon? Are you almost finished with Andy's leg?"

Woody wiped Andy's blood off his hands with one of his alcohol cleaning cloths, "Abby, you have that tricky glint in your eye. Come on, out with it. What's your plan?"

CHAPTER THIRTEEN

Very quietly and emotionally controlled she began, "It's too late and too dark. With luck, no one will be too observant at Camp Mercyville. We go to the morgue, and we borrow the uniforms of the two soldiers who died at the mine yesterday. We clean up and dress up in those uniforms, and then we carry Andy and Twitch back to camp as if they had too much to drink, and."

Aunt Abby exclaimed, "Woody! Stop looking at me that way! It's a good plan! I just know we can pull it off."

Woody chuckled, "Oh Abby, I love you with your secret machinations, but this time it won't be necessary."

Upset, Abby turned beet red, "And why not? We have to keep the tunnel a secret. If we don't, then everyone who helps us and depends on us will be in danger, and we will have to start all over again from scratch somewhere else."

Trying to keep a straight face, Woody grinned from ear to ear, "Ah Abby, who's the Union captain in charge of Camp Mercyville?"

Frustrated Abby replied, "I don't know probably some old stick in the mud ready to follow the letter of the fugitive slave law and can't be trusted. Why do you ask?"

Teasingly he joked, "I am shocked at your ignorance. Abby, this is the one time I know something before you do in Mercyville. Why Abby, you're slipping." Woody chuckled, "Because I know him, and so do you, and he would be offended knowing you called him an old stick in the mud." Woody proudly grinned from ear to ear.

Abby quickly put one plus one together and realized who Woody was talking about. Her beet red face turned into a happy grin, "Why you horse's petard! Why didn't you tell me Cousin Nick is in charge of the camp? I'd have dragged both Andy and Twitch over there as soon as the two of us got out of the tunnels."

Woody looked askance at her, "Right! And how would you explain to the entire community what the two of us were doing in the tunnels tonight? Hmm, do you want everyone in town thinking that the two of us were in the tunnels for romantic reasons? They might just believe it, but it would raise even more questions in the wrong places, like the mayor's office, and then we would have to shut down the operation."

Abby chuckled, "Your right, what do we do?" Exasperated, she sighed.

Woody claimed, "I believe what my grandfather taught me about the British Army will come in handy right now with the Union Army."

Abby looked questioningly at him, "Stop keeping me on pins and needles, come on out with it."

"My grandfather said if you want to keep a secret, hide it in a lie in plain sight. We are going to bring the two of them over to the base and help the guards find them without incriminating ourselves, of course."

Woody was beaming now. "We'll use my delivery wagon for these two very special editions to deliver at the station. Keep watch while I hitch up my wagon. I will be back in a few minutes."

While Abby waited, she lovingly wiped the dirt and grime off of Andy's face and kissed him on his cheek. With Twitch unconscious, she worried about his concussion. However, there was nothing she could do about it.

She heard Woody pull the delivery wagon up to the rear door. He poked his head in, "Abby, are they ready to go? You get the door, and I'll carry them out."

Woody came through the back door to pick up Twitch. Woody grunted from the dead weight as he slung Twitch over his shoulder. In a moment, he placed Twitch on his back in the delivery wagon. Woody paused to catch his breath.

He whispered to Abby, "We're doing alright. I didn't wake anyone in the neighborhood. So far so good."

He slipped back inside for Andy, "Abby, it's frigid outside, do you want a ride home?"

Abby was ready to leave and already wearing her gray wool coat and red scarf. Grinning she replied, "No, I'll lock up sweetie. I still have the spare key."

Woody gave her a good night, or rather, a good morning kiss, "Please do, and if anyone is up this early they will only see me making my early morning paper run. I threw a couple of bundles of today's edition into my delivery wagon. It'll make nice pillows for our two sleeping beauties, and I'll covered them with a tarp to hide them and keep them warm."

Woody gently lifted Andy up, and discovered Andy was light as a feather compared to Twitch. As soon as Woody carried Andy out the back door, Abby locked up and headed in the opposite direction out of the back alley.

Then he slowly headed the wagon team toward Camp Mercyville. It was a short and uneventful drive. He pulled up in front of the train station just short of the camp. Observing the guards from a distance, he was right that they were intently watching the camp perimeter on the other side of the Mercyville Train Station, and not watching the station.

Quietly, Woody pulled over to the station's telegraph office. With the station building between him and the guards, there was no way the guards could see him and they would not catch him dropping off this morning's special delivery.

Gently but quickly, he unloaded his two fragile special editions, Andy and Twitch, onto a platform waiting bench, and put a bundle of this morning's newspapers by the office door.

Catching his breath, he composed himself for the next step in his plan. Trying to restrain a grin, he ran to the edge of the platform facing the guards. Waving his arms and screaming, "Help! Guards! Guards! Help Me! Get a Surgeon! Help! Help Me! I found some wounded Union soldiers over here!"

Two young guards came running over, as the rest remained at their post, one of them demanded, "What's going on here? What's all the fuss?"

Woody intentionally babbled and acted hysterically, "Over here sir! I was delivering my papers when I discovered them! I think their hurt? I can't wake them, are they dead? Are they? Can you help them? Are you a surgeon?"

Woody figured if he kept asking questions and acting hysterical then the guards would not question him, and their paternal instincts would kick in. Sure enough, a guard's instincts took over, "Charlie, these guys are hurt bad! We got to get them to the surgeon!"

Pointing at Woody, "We're commandeering your delivery wagon!" Woody gladly obliged him.

The two guards loaded Andy and Twitch aboard the wagon. And then a guard climbed aboard the delivery wagon and sat next to Woody. The guard ordered him, "Drive straight through the main gate and up to the field hospital."

Woody sat there and did as the guard told him, and he was secretly delighted that the Union Army took over the rescue.

Return of the Dead

At the field hospital, Surgeon Lindquist was already there, ready and waiting to save Andy and Twitch's lives. Lindquist instructed the first-time stretcher-bearers how to lift the wounded soldiers onto the stretchers carefully and then led the way into the field hospital, dropping the flaps behind the last stretcher bearer.

Before anyone thought to ask him one too many questions, Woody started to roll out of camp on his delivery wagon, when he heard someone clear his throat from behind, and then he heard Nick's familiar voice, "Morning Woody. You thought you could get away with not waking me. Now, you should know better than that. Can I at least offer you a cup of coffee in gratitude for bringing them home?"

Woody grinned, "Sure Nick, and I have quite a tale to tell you."

Nick grinned, "I was hoping you would say that. By the way, who did you drop off for the surgeon?"

Woody sat silently as a young private ran over to them from the field hospital, and started babbling, "Captain! Captain! The surgeon told me to find you and tell you that they are both alive. They're two of the soldiers we lost at the mine. One woke up. I heard him say his name, it's Private Anders. He said Jacob is dead and he's got a twitch, and then he passed out again."

Nick stood there taking in the young private's avalanche of words. He restrained the fatherly joy and relief he felt in his heart for Andy and Twitch. He sighed heavily, "Woody come on down off that wagon, leave it there and walk with me. This morning, I think you have a lot of explaining to do. Even though it is still long before sunrise, this celebration calls for something good and strong to drink other than coffee."

By the time, Nick and Woody reached Nick's tent, word of the resurrection of their two dead comrades quickly spread throughout the entire camp.

Hearing all the commotion outside his tent, Digger woke up and discovered the good news about Andy and Twitch's resurrection. By the time, Nick and Woody arrived, Digger was already over to Nick's tent, sitting there with a jug of hard cider and three glasses already set up on Nick's table to toast their friend's resurrection.

Nick stepped into his tent, "Well Digger, I see you already heard the good news about Andy and Twitch."

Digger responded with a giant ear-to-ear grin, "I thought you might like to wet your whistle with a toast to our good fortune."

Nick nodded in agreement. "With Woody being here, it feels like old times again. Woody, thank you for bringing them home safe and sound to us. I just wish we could say the same for the two recruits we lost in that landslide."

Digger poured a drink for all three of them, and then passed the filled tin cups around for the toast. They all sadly nodded in agreement as Nick raised his tin cup, "To those we thought dead but returned and to those who died or will die because of this lousy Rebellion. They started it, but we will finish it. God Bless the Union."

After they toasted the return of their friends, Woody could not bring himself to tell them about Abby and the tunnels. So, he lied and told them his cover story - how he was delivering the special edition about the Rebellion when he found the two on the station platform. Both Nick and Digger did not believe him for one minute, but who were they to question an old friend's tall tale.

Nick, speculated, "We have a handful of murders on our hands. Five murders on the plantation and two recruits killed at the mine. Gentlemen, someone will hang for all those murders. However, right now the question is what are we going to do about the mayor, his conspirators and the rebel spies?"

Digger chimed in, "We have no real proof. Only speculation as to what the mayor's real plans are. Perhaps it would be best to wait until Twitch and Andy are awake. Maybe they found something in the mines."

That reminded Woody of what he found on Andy and Twitch when he bandaged and sutured them up.

Woody slowly removed a small but heavy looking leather pouch out of his pocket. He held it up for them to see as he spoke, "I think you two need to see what is in my little magic pouch here. I believe it just might tell you a great deal about what is going on in Mercyville. That is if you really want to stop the mayor and rebel spies before they can bring their plan to fruition."

The coins clunked when it hit the tabletop as Woody tossed the pouch towards Nick's side of the table.

Nick saw the seriousness in Woody's eyes and reached over to pick up the pouch. Woody, stopped Nick's hand with a gentle touch, "Nick I could have left these coins in Andy and Twitch's pockets for old Surgeon Lindquist to find. However, I thought you would prefer to have both bags before anyone in the field hospital saw the coins."

Woody dropped a second smaller pouch in Nick's hand. "I found all of these coins stuffed in their pockets. Consider for a moment, how half our medical staff was trained in the south, and the other half up here by surgeons who abandoned the Union to fight with the rebels. Only Twitch and Andy know where the rest of these coins are hidden, so I would tread very quietly with who I trusted with the knowledge of what is in those bags."

Nick felt the weight of the pouches and immediately knew it contained some coins inside of it. His first impulse was to dump the bag over onto the table for all to see. "Woody, who else knows about these pouches?"

Looking straight into Nick's eyes, Woody whispered, and again he lied, "Besides you and Digger, Andy and

Twitch, just me and no one else." However, Woody stopped himself from mentioning Abby.

Nick reached in and removed one gold coin. It happened to be tails. He read the raised lettering.

For the longest time, Nick twiddled the coin between his thumb and forefinger in deep thought, "There must be more of these, any ideas where they might be?"

Digger spoke up, "What about the twelve crates now buried in the Mines of Misery? That would explain why the mine entrance was dynamited. It was to keep us from getting our hands on the gold. What if this whole rebel spy conspiracy has been about gold?"

Woody smiled, "Look at the big picture, twelve chests of coins marked the Republic of Katz. Mercyville is strategically located between the Connecticut River and Bolton Notch."

Thinking aloud, Nick spoke up, "If Mercyville became the twelfth Confederate state then Governor Katz could block all armament, supply, and troop train movements through Eastern Connecticut. That would force all rail shipments through the Massachusetts northern route. And reroute shipments by sea around Cape Cod and through Long Island Sound to deliver to New York."

Woody agreed, "The Mayor's scheme sounds deviously simple and would hamper the Union war effort by delaying every New England war goods delivery over land through Connecticut."

Nick nodded in agreement and added, "Imagine what would happen if the Confederates could get a foothold in the northern states. The Union would appear to be fragmented and breaking up. Why this might even be enough to undermine our relations with the British and French. It would give the rebels the upper hand to finance their Rebellion."

Digger did not like what he heard, and angrily he suggested, "I only know we have rebel spies running amuck around here, and it is time to put an end to them. I say we go out and shoot the lot of them starting with those prisoners who shot the immigrant workers."

Nick, looked askance at Digger, "And what about the ones who buried you alive, would you let them live?"

Digger smiled a grin of satisfaction, "Andy and Private Sanders took care of most of them for me. From what the teamsters tell me, Sanders put on quite a show lining up a nice two-tiered firing squad to the detriment of the rebel spies as they tried to attack the wagons. My only regret is that Falsemouth didn't get shot along with the rebel spies."

Nick's ears perked up, "What was that about Private Falsemouth? Why do you want to shoot him?"

Digger disgustedly frowned as he told them his long story of what happened, "The night I disappeared, I saw

Falsemouth talking to Matthews when he was tied to the tree, and then I watched him slink away between the barns. I made the mistake of following Falsemouth by myself. Thinking back on it, he must have known I was following him because he led me on a wild goose chase through a bunch of back alleyways. I followed him, and eventually, he went into the new city hall."

Digger took a sip of hard cider, and continued, "Through the window, I could see Falsemouth arguing with Mayor Katz. I wasn't close enough to read their lips, but shortly Falsemouth came out and headed towards the cemetery road. I should have known he was going to waylay me as he ducked into the cemetery. I stupidly followed him in."

Digger made a fist and pounded the table as he said, "Wham! Someone hit me on the back of the head and stunned me."

Taking a deep breath, Digger continued, "Nick the weird thing is, they did not even ask me any questions. They already had the lid off that stone tomb and shoved me into it. I fought off four of them, but the fifth one hit me below the belt and ordered the other four to seal in that 'Damn Yankee.' I never heard such hatred in my whole life. I'm glad those rebel spies are dead."

Nick thought about Digger's story, "Do either of you know what happened to Falsemouth?"

Digger, sighed as he started to report about the mine, "We were at the old Misery Copper Mine waiting for Twitch, Jacob and Andy to come out from scouting the tunnels. I sent Sanders down to find out what was taking so long. That's when Sanders suddenly started screaming, Get back! Get Back! Run! Falsemouth's Got Dynamite!"

Nick half expected Digger to pound the tabletop again. Instead, Digger continued to narrate his report,

"Nick, I never saw recruits run so fast in my whole life. The earth shook, and the whole side of the quarry came down. At the time, along with Andy, Jacob, and Twitch, two recruits Harry Harrington and Salvador Smithers didn't make it out. I'll get their next of kin for you later today."

Nick nodded his head in agreement and said, "Thank you, Digger. I would appreciate that so I can notify their families as soon as possible and send their bodies home, please continue. I am interested in what happened next."

After taking another sip of hard cider, Digger related, "As the debris field cloud came down, we lost sight of Sanders in the dirt cloud, and I feared we lost him too. Fortunately, he reappeared and barely made it out alive."

Then Digger said proudly, "I got to give Sanders credit for his quick thinking. In all the commotion he almost caught up to Falsemouth by the horses, but Falsemouth was a tad quicker than Sanders. As Falsemouth was riding off, Sanders fired all six rounds from a Colt revolver at him. I'm not sure, but it looked like one of the shots winged Falsemouth."

Nick asked, "Where did Sanders get the revolver?"

Digger smiled, "Isaac gave Sanders one. I think it belonged to one of the rebels killed when they attacked the wagons."

Nick understood, "Oh, okay. Please continue."

Speaking proudly, Digger said, "Sanders was smart enough not to chase after Falsemouth. Instead, Sanders ran back to the debris field trying to dig everyone out. The rest of us could see it was useless. We knew we could not get to Andy, Jacob, and Twitch.

"But Sanders would not give up searching for the buried men. He was like a madman as he dug through the rubble. Sanders found the bodies of Harrington and Smithers near the edge of the debris field. They hadn't run fast enough, and just too much debris from the hill came down and crushed them.

"It took four men to pull Sanders off that rock pile and to calm him down. Sanders really cares about his comrades and seems to understand them instinctively. He quickly pulled himself together, and his men followed his lead as they dug out the remains of the two recruits."

Nick shook his head, "When you got back, I was devastated at the news of losing those men. I cursed the mayor and his rebel spies for killing them. Now that I know the whole story I promise you Digger that we will bring Falsemouth in and after a court-martial, he will hang as a traitor."

Nick continued, "As for the mayor and anyone else involved in this rebel scheme, we need to catch them, and I think the courts will find them guilty and they will be paid a visit by the hangman as well."

The three of them sat quietly ruminating on the present situation, when Nick stated, "Now first things first, do we give Sanders a medal or do we promote him? Or do we do both?"

Digger and Woody both grinned and agreed by putting their thumbs up to give Sanders a medal and a promotion to corporal.

Digger stared sternly at Woody, "Woody did you just re-enlist?"

Taken aback, Woody firmly stated, "No! I most certainly did not re-enlist. Furthermore, I have a newspaper to run, where words are more powerful than swords. Digger, you know the power of the press."

Digger mischievously teased, "In that case, if you want your vote to count, Woody, you had better enlist right now. I got me those papers on me somewhere. Give me a minute and I'll ..."

Woody bolted out of Nick's tent and headed towards the main gate. Chuckling Digger shouted after him, "Now

Woody you get back here! I found your paperwork! Nick, I do not know, I must be losing my touch or something. I keep losing recruits that way. I'm sorry Nick, I guess he decided to high tail it back to his printing presses."

Nick joked, "Don't worry Digger! Woody will be back, he forgot his delivery wagon." They both enjoyed a good laugh over it as did Woody when he returned to get his wagon.

TWO FACED TRAITOR

Nick Seriously Said, "Digger, we have some serious business to discuss. We need a twenty-four-hour guard around Andy and Twitch. I believe they are still in mortal danger, and before the day is over another attempt will be made on their lives."

Digger responded, "We can trust Sanders and his recruits. Something tells me all those boys have true hearts and would walk through fire for Sanders. As for the medical staff in the field hospital, I agree with Woody that one way or another every surgeon has either a direct or indirect connection with the southern doctors, who deserted to join the Rebellion."

Nick shook his head, "Digger, that's not necessarily true, the North has some fine schools too. Surgeon Lindquist immigrated from Sweden, and graduated from a European school, before teaching in New York. I trust him. However, I will leave the protection of Andy and Twitch in your hands and Sanders's hands as well."

Nick thought for a moment, "Let's make a big thing out of Sanders's actions on the field of combat. Write up a citation and promotion for Sanders to corporal, and I'll add my two cents seal of approval.

"Oh, Digger, before I forget, throw in a citation for the rest of his squad… Ah, let me think a minute. Make it for outstanding bravery in the face of the enemy."

Thoughtfully Nick added, "Now before I decide on our next course of action with the mayor, let's see if we can trap a few more of the mayor's rebel spies while Andy and Twitch are still in the field hospital. Here's the rumor I want you to spread about them …"

Nick leaned over and whispered the false rumor into Digger's ear and then added, "Remember, after you spread the rumor around camp, mention it at the field hospital. I trust Lindquist, but some of the other surgeons and aides may be rebel sympathizers."

"How you handle this, I leave up to you. Just make sure Sanders and his men are in on it, so they know what to expect and can act swiftly on the sly …"

Digger headed out to get things rolling. Nick leaned against his tent pole flipping one of Mayor Katz's gold coin in the air. Half to himself, he chuckled and could barely be heard under his breath saying, "You need lots of golden molasses to catch a big fat rebel like Katz."

Nick talking to himself added, "As for the golden hoard, retrieving the coins will have to wait until Andy and Twitch are up and about again."

He sighed and headed back to his tent to fill out the rest of his report to the President including Falsemouth's traitorous actions leading up to the death of the recruits.

Digger headed straight over to the Quartermaster's tent. He filled Birdy in on the plan and had him spread the rumor there. Next Digger headed on over to the Mess tent for a quick breakfast. He made sure the cooks and those on KP overheard the false rumor about Andy and Twitch stealing the gold, and then moving it out of the mines just before Falsemouth blew up the mine entrance.

He did not say the same thing in both places but only twisted the facts enough to make it more arguable. After all, for a good rumor to spread all you need is more than one version of it to give everyone something to disagree about. Otherwise, a rumor does not spread but dies. It is a simple matter of human nature. If you don't understand something, you ask someone about it and so on. Doing this makes rumors seem more urgent and helps to spread the rumor even faster. He chuckled at the simplicity of the captain's plan.

By the time Digger finished eating he had figured half the camp would hear the rumor by mid-day and the rest by early afternoon. That did not leave him much time to get Sanders in place to make the plan work.

Digger stopped in to visit Private Sanders, who seemed in charge of the other recruits at their bivouac. Most of the recruits were still sleeping off yesterday's expedition. However, Digger was in luck, Sanders sat by a barrel, eating his breakfast of sausage and egg along with coffee and a biscuit. Sanders stood up as Digger approached. "Nice breakfast you have there, Sanders. Let's sit while you finish eating. I have some good news for you. Have you heard about the two soldiers rescued from the mine this morning?"

Angela's heart did a double beat, and she prayed beyond all belief that one was Andy. She took a short breath and as calmly as she could in her fake voice, "Ah, no sir, is there good news?"

"I'll say there is! Private Anders and Lieutenant Twitch showed up at the front gate this morning. As soon as you finish breakfast, we have a great deal of work to do to protect them."

She almost screamed for joy that Andy was alive. Instead, she sat there grasping her coffee cup until it hurt her fingers. She grinned from ear to ear at the good news.

Taking a deep breath, Angela said as Sanders, "Sergeant if there is anything you want me and my squad to do for them, you just name it, and we will do it."

He leaned over and whispered into Sanders' ear. "Sanders, I'm glad you said that because here's the plan … The captain wants your squad to be the guard unit around the hospital tent, where they are recovering. No one in or out, do you understand?"

When she heard his plan, she could not help but smile, and her eyes got big in anticipation of being near Andy again. However, she came up with an even better plan to protect Andy and Twitch. She guardedly replied, "Yes sir, I will gather my recruits together and have them in place as quickly as possible to guard the hospital tent."

Hearing Sanders enthusiastic response, Digger was pleased and gladly replied, "I'm glad I can rely on you and your recruits. Now I have to get going to follow through with my part of the plan. I will be over there to check on things in an hour or two, so I suggest you get your men up and moving if we are to pull this off."

Angela's squad did not have a bugler to call Reveille, so she did the next best thing. She took her empty plate and tossed the rest of the wretched coffee into their campfire.

Angela as Private Sanders went from tent to tent repeatedly banging her empty tin coffee cup on her tin plate and shouting as loud as possible, "Revelry! Revelry!

Surprise Inspection! Surprise Inspection! Everybody Ah-ten! Hut!" She kept yelling it over and over again until she became hoarse and sounded like a Private Sanders should sound.

All twenty-four of her loyal recruits lined up the best they could. Most of them were half awake and disheveled, but standing at attention in line. Yes, some had trouble getting dressed, and their shirts were not buttoned up correctly. However, they were all lined up and at attention for their Private Sanders. "Alright, men gather around me and listen carefully, have I got a mission for you, today."

As soon as they surrounded her, she realized the tallest recruit was beside her. She poked him in the ribs, "Stretch, you're the lookout, poke your head up and keep watch. Let me know if anyone is trying to listen in or comes within earshot." He proudly stood guard.

Angela did not realize it, but she just assigned her first nickname to one of her men. "Alright men, I have good news and bad news, Private Anders and Lieutenant Twitch are alive and recovering in the field hospital." Her squad cheered wildly.

"What's the bad news, sir?" Momentarily, she was taken aback by being called, "Sir."

She continued, "I'll get to that in a moment. We have successfully pulled off one campaign against the rebels, and now we have a new mission. This time it is to perpetrate a ruse on the rebel sympathizers and spies and to secure the field hospital.

The captain fears the field hospital is a hotbed of coals - I mean rebel spies, and someone there might try to do them in. So, we have to infiltrate." She could not believe that every recruit gasped in unison.

"Here's our plan to save them, remember, you all play an important role … Now listen up."

She stopped talking, and looked up at Stretch, "Can you hear me up there Stretch?"

"Yes sir, no intruders nearby sir. "

"Good, come on down and join the huddle. Alright men, let's get down to business. Here's how I figure we can infiltrate the field hospital…"

Angela was feeling a bit like a mother hen addressing her baby chicks, she said to her squad, "I'm afraid you're going to have to throw up."

She heard a retching sound, "Not here Winslow after we eat breakfast in the mess tent! We are going to pretend to be sick from food poisoning so we can fill the ward, and be there when the rebel spies try to kill Andy and Twitch. Now, let's get over to the Mess tent, and I will tell you the rest of my plan. Any questions?"

"Sir, do we need to bring buckets with us?"

"No, it's supposed to be spontaneous. Now let's get some breakfast."

~ ~ ~

Eventually, Digger finished spreading the word about Andy and Twitch being in the field hospital and the gold theft. He hightailed it over to the field hospital to spread the rumor to the surgeons and aides.

As Digger entered the field hospital tent, almost immediately, he noticed most of the beds in the ward were full of his sick recruits, which he thought was rather odd.

A bald but bearded Surgeon stepped up to happily greet Digger. With a hearty but a bit extra firm handshake the surgeon quickly rattled on, "Good morning, you must be Sergeant Palgrave, a pleasure to meet you at last. I am Surgeon Gallstone, ah, I mean Surgeon Janus Julius Gallstone. I just arrived this morning and am covering for Surgeon Lindquist, who is tied up with his assistants elsewhere."

He quickly added, "I assume you're here to check on all your men. We seem to have had a bit of food poisoning in the Mess tent today. I was told something about bad bacon. I do believe Private Sanders can fill you in, he's right over here." Gallstone pointed toward the other end of the tent where Andy and Twitch should have been.

Digger paused before he answered the surgeon because food poisoning was not part of the captain's plan. He worried that it was all starting to go wrong. Now a bit unnerved and taken off guard. He hesitatingly responded, "Oh, ah yes, I would like to check on them at once. Ah, that is why I am here. Ah, please do lead the way. Ah, how are they doing?"

Gallstone grinned from ear to ear, "Oh they'll be fine in a couple of hours, nothing severe. I am just keeping them here for observation. Excuse me for a moment. My aide just signaled me he needs my help to prepare some vitamin shots for the two unconscious men."

Digger finally got away from the surgeon and quickly moved past the beds looking for Sanders. Finally, he found Sanders, who was faking a sick stomach in the cot next to Andy, "What do you think you're doing private? I told you to place your recruits around the tent strategically."

Answering him as Sanders, "But they are around the tent, sergeant?"

"I didn't mean inside it, I meant around the outside."

Angela knew she was caught in her slight misdirection, "Ah, we all messed up, and we are here now … Do you want us to leave?"

Digger replied, "No, it's too late for that, let me plant the rumor with the surgeon, about those two trying to make off with the gold stash, but first, I need to see how Andy and Twitch are doing."

Before Angela could say anything else, Digger turned and lifted Andy's bed sheet. Only to be startled at finding Winslow staring back at him and not Andy, "Hi Sergeant Palgrave!"

Digger quickly dropped the sheet and angrily turned to Private Sanders, "Where's Andy?"

Sanders, sheepishly replied, "We put him with Twitch." Then quickly added, "Don't worry, they're both safe and sound with the rest of the squad someplace secret. We hid them where nobody would think to look for them."

Digger rather loudly inquired, "And where would that be? May I ask?"

Angela whispered, "Shh, that's confidential sergeant, I promised the squad not to tell anyone, not even you or the captain. The less you know, the better. Besides, the canvas walls have ears. Why this morning, every hour on the hour, someone kept creeping up and standing outside the wall by their beds. I've got two of my best men on it, and expect them to ..."

Digger was about to interrupt Sanders when a scuffle ensued outside the tent. He heard a loud smack as someone was hit and landed hard on the side of the tent. Half of the supposedly sick squad members jumped off their cots and charged out of the ward to join in the fray. The rest stayed put on guard.

Upset by the failure of Nick's plan, Digger stomped out only to discover the squad was pig-piled on top of someone. Pulling them off, one by one, he finally uncovered the interloper at the bottom of the pile.

The interloper appeared bruised and battered, with two black eyes and a broken nose. "Well, I'll be! It's my old friend Falsemouth! Gentlemen, you do great work, you caught a rebel spy and traitor. I am very proud of all of you."

Digger reached down and with one of his big hands grabbed Falsemouth by the shoulder. Falsemouth winced from the unbelievable shoulder pain as Digger grasped a firm hold on Falsemouth's already wounded shoulder.

"Well, what do you know! It looks as if Sanders did shoot you after all." Digger demanded to know from Falsemouth, "Who bandaged you up? Who was the surgeon that helped you? Who? Tell me now!"

Falsemouth whimpered as Digger squeezed his shoulder and whined, "As I'd tell the likes of you anything! You overgrown oaf!"

Angered, Digger could not help himself as he gave a good hard squeeze to Falsemouth's bandaged shoulder, Falsemouth groaned and swooned, as Digger declared, "Falsemouth, you're under arrest for desertion, attempted murder, and treason."

With one hand, Digger quickly tossed Falsemouth to the squad almost knocking three of them over. "Take Falsemouth away, and make sure he gets to a cell alive. I want to see him ..."

Digger was cut off in midsentence when a louder commotion broke out, but this time it was inside the hospital tent, it sounded like another scuffle. He lamented, "Now what?"

Quickly Digger charged back into the field hospital tent just in time to discover the bearded Surgeon Janus Gallstone and one of his aides fighting with the other half of Diggers' supposedly sick squad members. It was just as Digger feared, the recruits were out of control.

He was about to shout out an order to stop when Private Sanders smashed a porcelain bedpan over Surgeon Gallstone's head knocking him unconscious. Almost at the same time, Winslow swung a crutch as he would a baseball bat, and Gallstone's aide met the same fate falling over backward onto a bed. Instead of a home run, though, Winslow had knocked the aide out cold.

Digger shouted out, "Everyone freeze right where you are! What's going on in here?"

Sanders, still holding onto the porcelain bedpan, grinned and replied, "The surgeon had two needles: one for Twitch and the other for Andy. He was trying to inject Andy with something first. So, we stopped him."

Digger looked at all of them in disgust, and started yelling, "He's a surgeon! You bunch of dumb misfits! His name's Gallstone! He's supposed to use needles to inject patients with vitamins and other medicines. Now get Gallstone onto a cot, and locate Surgeon Lindquist to attend to them."

Exasperated and thinking about being busted back to corporal, again, Digger muttered, "I will be lucky if all of you are court-martial for attacking our new surgeon.

Maybe I'll get recruits who actually follow orders." Then he shouted, "Now get Gallstone onto a cot! Now, move him!"

Privates Sanders, Stretch, and Winslow were closest to Surgeon Gallstone, so they reached down to lift him up onto the cot. Accidently, Winslow's sleeve buttons brushed against the surgeon's face and tangled in his beard. Angela pretending to be Sanders ordered, "On the count of three we all lift. One. Two. Three!"

As they lifted Gallstone, his beard came off attached to Winslow's buttons. Stretch shouted, "Hey, Gallstone's wearing a fake beard. Who is that? He sure looks familiar!"

Angela looked down to see what all the fuss was about, and she burst out laughing. Finally, she came to her senses and remembered she was Private Sanders. She grabbed Mayor Katz's dislodged beard and pulled it completely off. She waved it around high above her cap to show it off to everybody.

In her best Sanders voice, she proclaimed, "It's Mayor Katz, we didn't recognize him because he shaved his head and was wearing this false beard. Digger! I think my squad should be cleared of assaulting an officer because he is no surgeon. He is a traitor! Now we can arrest the Mayor, for the attempted murder of Andy and Twitch."

Digger grinned from ear-to-ear and announced, "Great job Corporal Sanders. You and your men are going to arrest these rebel conspirators, but first, we have to find the real surgeons, to attend to these two. The last thing we want is for them to die before they get to the gallows."

Angela as Sanders, "Digger! Did you just field promote me to corporal?" Grinning, he nodded his head, yes, "Now Corporal, I strongly urge you to order your men to search Camp Mercyville for the missing surgeon and his aide. Otherwise, Sanders, you will be a private again in the blink of an eye."

Angela, immediately, started issuing orders to her men, who quickly vanished from the field hospital tent in search of the surgeon and his aide.

The squad searched the tents around the field hospital all to no avail. However, their search of the surgeon in the Officers area turned up the surgeon and both of his assistants. They were stripped of their uniforms and dressed only in their long johns. The men were gagged and hogtied to their cots.

~~~

Later that day, Andy and Twitch woke up in the old town hall and did not have the vaguest idea how they ever got there. At least, not until Digger showed up, and told them that Falsemouth was a rebel conspirator, and how he blew up the Misery Copper Mine with dynamite to collapse the mine entrance trying to kill Jacob, Andy, and Twitch.

Then Digger filled Andy in on how Falsemouth had tried a second time to get at and kill Andy and Twitch in the field hospital. But once again Falsemouth had been
~~~

stopped by the brave and seemingly fearless Private Sanders, who had earned a well-deserved field promotion to corporal.

Andy listened to Digger go on and on and wasn't paying much attention to the discourse. His ears perked up when he heard he would get a three-day pass, as soon as he's discharged from the field hospital. After Andy heard about the leave, all he thought of was seeing Angela.

Digger digressed about as many of the details he remembered to make the tale more interesting. There was a gentle knocking on the room doorframe interrupting Digger's discourse.

Andy looked up to discover it was Angela in her brand-new pink spring dress. She also brought a new clean uniform for Andy with the compliments of Birdy.

Quickly, tossing Andy's dirty boots and new uniform on the dresser, she ran to Andy. They embraced and kissed in front of Digger, who blushed three shades of red.

Fortunately, for Angela, neither Andy nor Digger noticed the tips of the toes of Sanders's army boots peeking out from beneath her hemline every time she took a step.

While still embracing him, "Andy you have to promise me you're not going to die again on me like that. I couldn't stop crying because I thought I'd lost you."

They heard someone downstairs on the main floor as the back door slammed shut. Soon Nick popped his head into the room, "Good! I see you're both up and about. The surgeon said you should be ready to return to your duties in a day or two."

Twitch, chimed in, "Other than seeing double I'm fine, though I would feel better in my cot."

Nick smiled, 'Twitch, that is between you and Surgeon Lindquist. I'll send him around as soon as I get back to camp.

"May I have a minute with Andy, Miss Fishkill-Katz? As soon as I finish talking to him, you can get back to caring for him as you were doing when I arrived." Andy and Angela both blushed, as did Digger. "Andy, how's your leg healing up?"

Andy got out of bed and gingerly walked around a bit, "The surgeon said my stitches are healing up nicely. We don't know who sutured me up, but whoever sutured me up saved my life. As long as I don't run around a lot, I can return to duty."

"Alright, why don't you get dressed and return to base with me, I have a carriage out front."

Something was nagging on Nick's mind, "Andy, Twitch, when you both opened the crate, did you find any paperwork in it?"

He paused before continuing, "With the prisoners not talking, we don't have any real evidence against Mayor Katz. His lawyer claims the gold coins with the mayor's face stamped on them is a rebel conspiracy to implicate the mayor when in reality, the mayor is innocent of all charges.

"As for the mayor's attempted murder of the two of you, His lawyer claims that the mayor only dressed up because he was worried about your health, and wanted to make sure you were getting the proper care."

Everyone gasped, and then Nick added, "All we need is one piece of hard evidence linking him to the rebels."

Everyone was stunned by Nick's revelation, for all of them thought the "Republic of Katz" gold coins were enough evidence to convict Katz of treason.

Disappointedly, Angela pulled Andy's uniform off the bureau and knocked his boots onto the floor. The waterproof parcel clunked out of his boot. Nick bent over and picked it up, "Andy what's this?"

All excited Andy yelled, "Twitch! We forgot about the waterproof package. Go on captain open it up. I'm dying to know what's in it."

Digger exclaimed, "Maybe it's what we need to convict Katz! Here use my knife, Nick."

The bundle was heavily sealed in wax. Even though Digger's pocketknife was super sharp, Nick had a hard time cutting through the wrapper and bindings.

TWO FACED TRAITOR

Finally, Nick pulled out a packet of tightly bound papers. Undoing the bindings, he unfolded the documents, which opened everyone's eyes to Katz's traitorous actions.

The pouch contained design and delivery receipts for the gold coins and were all signed by Aloysius T Katz. Also, a letter from the Provisional President of the Confederacy, Jefferson Davis, to Katz dated February 18, 1861.

It commended him on his audacious plan to split the Union and promoted him to General Aloysius T. Katz. Nick looked at the date and exclaimed, "Well I'll be a monkey's uncle! That must have been one of the first executive orders Jefferson Davis signed after he was sworn in."

They also found maps of the Republic of Katz. Unfolding the Republic of Katz maps, everyone gasped at the territory of the new Republic of Katz, the 12th Confederate State splitting the State of Connecticut in two, and making Mercyville its new capital city.

Turning the maps over, they discovered scrawled timelines and battle agendas for every rebel attack to take place and identified the leaders of the attacks.

In other words, it was General Aloysius T. Katz's full battle plans also approved and signed by the Provisional President of the Confederacy Jefferson Davis and dated February 18, 1861.

Everyone felt good knowing they now had enough evidence to convict and send Aloysius T. Katz to the gallows along with his conspirators and the rebel spies.

Nick said, "Well we better get going Digger, we now have too much paperwork to complete. Twitch I have a wagon, do you want a lift back to your tent?"

"Of course, Nick, I think my cot is more comfortable then this makeshift bed of boxes."

As soon as they were gone, Andy and Angela thought they would finally have some time alone, but they were wrong. Less than a minute later, they heard the workmen show up downstairs to convert the old town hall into the new Camp Mercyville HQ.

Nick and Digger dropped Twitch off back at his tent to rest up and recover. Then the two got to work on their paperwork. Digger a bit confounded said, "You know Nick, I am going to have to have a long talk with Sanders. I can't seem to find his enlistment paperwork to change his rank to corporal."

I hope you have enjoyed

Andy Anders and the Rebel Spies

Please tell your friends on social media

how much you have enjoyed this book.

To discover more about the

Adventures of Andy Anders

Check Out

allenalright.com

Thank you

Allen Alright

CHAPTER FOURTEEN

www.ingramcontent.com/pod-product-compliance
Lightning Source LLC
Chambersburg PA
CBHW030017200726

48283CB00012B/666